WITCH WAY TO SECRETS AND SORCERY

THE WITCH WAY MYSTERIES - BOOK 6

JANE HINCHEY

AUTHOR'S NOTE

Hey there! Welcome to a whirlwind of whimsy and wonder in my Witch Way Mysteries. If you've got a soft spot for the supernatural, you're in for a real treat.

This is your gateway to a world where magic and mystery intertwine. The Witch Way series has now woven its full tale, but the magic doesn't stop here. For news on my latest adventures and stories, don't forget to sign up for my newsletter.

Janehinchey.com/subscribe

Are you ready to conjure up some fun and unravel a few bewitching puzzles? I'll see you on the other side!

xoxo
Jane

ABOUT THIS BOOK

Tiny the giant fairy is intent on making life difficult for the residents of Whitefall Cove. But what happens when the cranky mechanic turns up dead in her garage?

Tiny and I have something in common. We share a birthday. So when a mysterious gift turns up on my doorstep that could have had me joining Tiny in the ever-after, I'm immediately suspicious. Add to that Tiny's death was staged to look like an accident and I'm convinced foul play was involved.

While I'm busy searching for clues, Gran is busy creating havoc at her new role as Advanced Potion's teacher at Drixworths Academy of Witchcraft and Wizardry. She's already on her third warning and I fear the powers that be will not be embracing her unorthodox teaching methods anytime soon.

When another body drops, coincidentally sharing a birthday with Tiny and I, I have a sneaking suspicion the killer will not quit until I'm dead. With my birthday celebrations on hold, I call the murder club to order—we have a mystery to solve and a killer to catch.

Since Gran had started her position at Drixworths Academy for Witchcraft and Wizardry, I'd started measuring my days in caffeine levels. And today was shaping up to be a level five. Possibly a six, but hey, the day was still young. Cradling my freshly refilled cup in my hands I leaned back, balancing on the rear two legs of the old kitchen chair on my front deck and resting my bare feet on the railing. The sky was awash with pinks and oranges; the colors clashing together in vivid imagery, like oil dropped into water.

"Are you even listening to me?" Gran's voice squawked through my phone.

"Yes," I reassured her, lying through my teeth. Gran had been gunning for the role of new headmistress at Drixworths since Izzy Higginbottom rather abruptly resigned. I say resigned, but I suspect the powers that be told her to leave voluntarily or be fired. When a rift had opened to another dimension in Whitefall Cove a couple of months ago, Izzy had not managed the situation well. In fact, her lies and cover-ups had made things worse. So when the vacancy for the position of headmistress was announced, Gran was all in. I'm not sure if it was a good thing or not that she didn't get the role—instead, they offered her a part-time teaching position. Advanced potions. That was six weeks ago, and I'd seen a slow decline in Drixworths enthusiasm for their new employee ever since.

First, it had been the grumbles about Gran's attire. She liked to dress in outfits not befitting an eighty-year-old woman. For Gran, crop tops, sequins, tutus, and fishnet stockings were the norm, not to mention her staple bedazzled Ugg boots. Then there had been the grumbles about class content. Gran had taught them a potion that would turn anyone who ingested it into a toad for twenty-four hours. Naturally, all the students had immediately gone home and slipped the potion to their parents. Gran was now on probation. Not that she seemed to care.

"Gran, I think you should follow the direction they have given you for the class. After all, that is what they're paying you for." And that direction had been textbook. No deviation. No ad-libbing.

"Hogwash." She scoffed. "They hired me for my experience. I want to teach these witches things they won't learn in any old spell book."

"You're asking for trouble." I idly watched a seagull come in to land on my gate post, watched it watching me, cocking its head to see if I had any food, then uttering a loud squawk before taking flight once more. Archie made a *mreet mreet* sound from his position on the deck next to my chair and I reached down to ruffle the fur behind his ear. "No hunting the wildlife remember?" I told him.

"What was that?" Gran asked.

"Nothing. I was talking to Archie. Look Gran, I don't think you should do the wide-eye potion—it's asking for trouble. Try to teach them something that will not lead to mischief and mayhem. Stick to the curriculum and the antidote to common poisons."

"But what witch or wizard wouldn't want the ability to not need sleep? Think how useful that would be—especially at exam time!"

"Gran—" I warned, but she cut me off. "Gotta go. I'll let you know how it goes." And she hung up.

Sighing, I drained my coffee and brought the chair back onto all four legs with a thunk. Mornings were my favorite time of day, coffee on the deck watching the sunrise. Except when Gran called with her next brilliant plan for class, shattering my peace and quiet. Hence the two cups of coffee already under my belt with the promise of more to come. Heading inside I washed my cup and left it on the sink to dry then headed upstairs to shower.

My assistant, Wendy, was opening The Dusty Attic bookstore today while I ran some errands and took the day off for my birthday. Tonight, my boyfriend, local Detective Jackson Ward, and I would celebrate with a sunset cruise, but this morning I'd been tasked with picking up a new oil filter for Gran's car. Jackson had volunteered to replace it for Gran, who ran her poor car ragged. The only fluid she put in it was fuel. Not oil. Not water. Not any other essential lubricant a car needs to keep its engine running. Jackson had noticed the clunking noise last time Gran had driven out to the lighthouse cottage to visit and had volunteered to do a mini service on her vehicle. I had no complaints about seeing Jackson in grease-stained jeans, an oily rag, and sweat running down his brow.

That particular vision lodged itself in my brain and stuck with me as I drove to Tiny's garage half an hour later. Tiny was anything but tiny. Despite being a fairy, she was a big unit, tall, wide, and intimidating. Take everything you imagine a fairy to be, then flip it. Pulling into the garage's parking lot I eyeballed Archie who was in his usual spot on the passenger seat.

"Stay in the car, okay?"

"*Mreow.*" I wasn't sure if his response was a protest or agreement. "If you start poking around

Tiny's garage you'll get grease in your fur and you know what that means. A bath. So keep your furry butt in the seat." Climbing out I stood with my hands on hips and squinted at the garage before me. The roller door was up, revealing the workshop inside. A yellow car was up on the hoist, a radio was blaring seventies tunes and a string of curses turned the air blue. Literally. When Tiny cussed, her breath came out blue, leaving little indigo clouds in the air. And she hates it. Which begs the question, *why cuss then?* But one thing I knew about Tiny was that she was one stubborn fairy and once she had her mind set on something, there was no changing it, so I figured she'd decided cussing was for her, blue breath and all.

Crossing to the workshop I cupped my hands around my mouth and shouted, "Tiny!"

There was a clunk, a curse, then Tiny stepped out from beneath the vehicle, a filthy rag pressed to her forehead. Spotting me, she narrowed her eyes and approached. "What?"

"Happy birthday," I smiled. Tiny and I may share a birthday, but I've learned from past experience that she doesn't appreciate having a birthday twin.

Her eyes narrowed to slits. "What?" She repeated, ignoring my mention of her birthday.

Smile fading, I dug into the back pocket of my jeans and pulled out the scrap of paper Jackson had written the part he needed on. Holding it out I asked, "do you have this in stock?"

Snatching the paper from me she squinted at it while I tilted my head back, looking up at her. She really was a giant. She had to be over seven feet tall. I wondered where she bought her clothes, or if she had to have them especially made. I usually saw her in coveralls, much like the filthy pair she was wearing today. Her wings were nowhere in sight and I figured they were tucked in the back, safe from the grease and oil in the workshop. Shifting my weight from one foot to the other I was now regretting my multiple cups of coffee start to the day as my bladder reached full capacity. I had two options. Hold it or use the garage's bathroom... although judging by the state of Tiny's garage I imagined the bathroom wouldn't meet any hygiene codes. But still, when a girl needed to go, beggars couldn't be choosers.

"Is it okay if I use your bathroom?" I asked. Tiny curled her hand into a fist, crushing the scrap of paper into a ball. "Does this look like a public restroom, huh?" She snapped, flinging the scrap of paper at my feet and pivoting on one heel she headed back into the workshop. For a giant fairy, she moved fast. Snatching up the paper, I hurried after her.

"But you have the oil filter, right?" I called, losing sight of her as I stepped from the bright sunlight into the dim recesses of the garage. I stopped, allowing my eyes to adjust, listening as Tiny rummaged around in the back—hopefully searching for the oil filter Jackson requested.

"Tiny! Where you at?" A voice yelled from behind me, making me jump. I hadn't heard anyone approach over the noise of the radio.

"Back." Came Tiny's response. A slim man in his forties walked past, nodded his head in greeting. He looked tired, his shoulders slumped, his jeans worn, his shirt fraying at the edges. I watched as he dug into his back pocket and pulled out a wad of cash. Okay, a wad was an exaggeration, but a few bills at least.

"You're late, Weaver," Tiny growled, snatching the notes from the man and counting them out in her big beefy hands. "You're twenty short."

"What? No way. There's a hundred there. I double-checked it myself." He protested, a hint of anger creeping into his voice. His hands curled into fists, then relaxed, as if realizing the futility of starting a fistfight with Tiny was a bad idea. Tiny held up four twenties and waved them in his face. "Forgot how to count did you moron?" She slapped the twenties against his forehead, and he winced. I felt awful for the way Tiny was belittling him.

"There was a hundred there and you know it." He protested. He pointed to a vehicle parked to the far left of the garage, draped in a tarp, "If you'll just let me have my truck I can get my produce to market and earn the money I owe you. We'll be all paid up in no time."

Tiny was already shaking her head. "Not how it works. No payment. No truck. Let me see." She tapped her lip and gazed up at the ceiling, deep in thought, "Minus this eighty, plus the fifty late fee, you still owe me..." she paused then fixed him with a smirk. "Twelve hundred and thirty dollars."

"What?" His voice went up several octaves. "My bill was a thousand! How can it be twelve hundred and thirty?"

"Interest." Tiny held up a meaty paw and counted off her fingers. "Late fees."

I could see the exact moment that the man called Weaver realized he was well and truly screwed. Defeat was written all over him, his entire body sagged with it, his eyes were dull with it and my heart went out to him. I could only surmise he'd had some mechanical emergency with his truck, Tiny had repaired it for him but wouldn't let him have it back until he'd paid up, in full. But he wasn't in a financial position to do that. In silence, he shuffled away.

Tiny stood with hands on hips, a smirk curling her lip. "Why don't you go ask your fox buddies for a loan?" She jeered, then under her breath, "Friggin shifters."

She swung her head my way and pinned me with her impossibly purple eyes. They were incredibly stunning but oh so cold. Tiny was not a fairy to be messed with and a shiver danced up my spine—but that could be because I badly need to pee. Clenching my knees I curled my lips into a smile and prompted, "Oil filter?"

"Right." She nodded, shoved the cash Weaver had given her down the front of her coveralls and returned to her search for the oil filter. The rear of the workshop housed shelves stuffed full of boxes and various car parts. From where I stood there appeared to be no order to her system, everything was a cluttered mess, but I figured Tiny had it set up exactly how she wanted it and I would keep any thoughts otherwise to myself. She rummaged some more, snagged a box smeared in grease from the back of the top shelf, and peered at it, holding it close to her face while she read the print that was mostly obscured by dirty fingerprints. With a nod to herself, she turned my way. *Yes!* Reaching into my purse I was getting ready to pay for the filter when Tiny's phone rang and she changed direction, diverting to the small office leading off the workshop floor. I sagged in disappointment while my bladder screamed.

Deciding I'd take the chance and risk Tiny's wrath, I hurried toward the door next to the office, the one with a "ladies" sign stuck to it. Tiny's back was to me as she snatched up the phone and I slipped into the bathroom. Through the wall I heard her bark, "Tiny's

Garage." I marveled that she got as much business as she did considering her overall demeanor but Jackson had told me she was one of the best mechanics in town.

Sliding down my jeans, I sat, unabashedly listening through the wall as I peed as silently as possible.

"Mathis, I told you already, not interested." A pause as the person on the other end of the phone, presumably Mathis, responded. "How much?" Tiny's voice held an element of surprise. "Well now, that is a very lucrative offer." Another pause. "But the answer is still no. Yeah, yeah, yeah, I know I told you I was interested but things have changed man. I got me something worth staying in Whitefall Cove for." My own brows rose at that. As far as I knew, Tiny lived alone in a ramshackle house directly across the street from her garage. The garage, and working on cars, was her life. Was it worth that much she'd never leave it? Possibly. I wondered if Mathis was offering to buy the garage from her—I could understand why she wouldn't sell, what would she do with herself if she didn't have the workshop and the enjoyment of tinkering on cars?

"Good luck with the race this weekend. I'll be watching. On tv." She clarified. Then hung up. And now I knew I was busted because I had to flush and Tiny may be a huge unit but she's not stupid. Deciding it best to rip this particular band-aid off fast, I flushed, washed my hands, vetoed the filthy hand towel hanging next to the basin, and wiped my hands on my jeans instead. I opened the door to find Tiny waiting for me. She wasn't pleased. Thrusting the oil filter against my chest so hard I staggered back, she glowered at me.

"Fifty." She snapped.

It was my turn to feel the same outrage Weaver had. Jackson had told me the filter would be thirty dollars, tops.

"Thirty." I counter-offered, not buying into Tiny's BS. Her brows pulled down, her lips thinned, and she loomed over me. I swallowed, my brief flash of bravado fleeing like a thief in the night. Before she could up the price to a hundred I squeaked, "Fifty it is," and held out a fifty-dollar note. She snatched it from me and shoved it down the front of her coveralls with the rest of her cash and I clutched the grimy oil filter box to my chest, stepped around her, and hurried out of the workshop without another word, almost running into Roxanne Mann as I did so.

"Slow down there," Roxanne held up both hands and took a hard step to the right to avoid colliding with me and the greasy box in my hands. As it was, my shirt was now smudged with a combination of grease and dust and my hands were filthy too.

"Sorry." I apologized, "I'd avoid Tiny today if I were you, she's in a bit of a mood."

Roxanne sneered, "Isn't she always?" and continued inside. It wasn't until I was in my car, the filter on the floor in the back, that it hit me as odd that Roxanne Mann would frequent Tiny's garage. Roxanne is Carson Singh's fiancee, and Carson is loaded. The guy probably wipes his butt with hundred-dollar bills he's that rich. Why then would his fiancee be taking her car to Tiny's garage when there are more top end garages in Whitefall Cove? And cleaner ones. Grabbing a tissue I scrubbed at my dirty hands but the grease had stuck. With a quick motion of my fingers, a wave of magic danced across my skin, taking the dirt and grime with it as the magic sparkled and died away. I upped my fantasy of Jackson in greasy jeans and sweat to now being topless to make up for the indignity of having to deal with Tiny. It was worth it.

TWO

"I have a solution," Gran said.

"Thank goodness." I kept my eyes glued on Jackson, who, true to my fantasies was stripped to the waist, denim jeans clinging in all the right places, sweat glinting off satin skin as he worked on Gran's car under the midday sun. Gran and I admired his work from my back deck, sweet tea in hand. I rarely sat out the back, but even the lighthouse and ocean could not rival today's view. After my successful mission to Tiny's garage this morning, Jackson had surprised me by swinging the day off, saying he'd work on Gran's car first to keep her safe on the roads, and then we'd have the rest of the day to ourselves. I wasn't sure servicing her car would make her any safer on the roads but I didn't want to burst his optimistic bubble so I'd smiled and nodded and agreed it was a wonderful idea.

"It involves fire." She added.

I almost spit out my sweet tea. "Absolutely not."

Gran sighed and rolled her eyes. "You didn't even hear me out."

"I didn't have to. If it involves fire or home-brewed alcohol, the answer is no."

"But it's your birthday Harper, you need to have a party." Her pout was real, as were the crossed arms. Gran could rival a four-year-old when it came to sulking.

"Gran," I sighed, "we've talked about this. No party. Jackson and I are having a romantic dinner tonight. Just the two of us."

"But-" she protested, but I cut her off. "No. Do you want me to tell Jackson to forget about your car?"

"No." She mumbled, temporarily defeated. I bit back a smile. Nothing defeated Gran for long and I knew if she had her way my birthday celebrations would snowball into an event of gargantuan proportions. Another year into my thirties was not something I wanted to celebrate. In my twenties, I thought I'd be married at thirty and having my first child at thirty-one. Thirty-two tops. Here I was with thirty-three barreling towards me and nothing but an ex-fiancee to show for it. Life had not gone to plan, but I couldn't really complain. I had a sexy cop for a boyfriend, I lived in the lighthouse cottage on the bluff and I had my own bookstore. Life was pretty good.

Leaning back in my deck chair I took another sip of sweet tea and continued my perusal of Jackson behind the lens of my sunglasses. Gran was stretched out on a towel in the sun, wrinkled skin glistening with sunscreen, while she flicked through the pages of a fashion magazine, making noises of delight when she found something she liked. It had been a turbulent year since my return to Whitefall Cove, but at this exact moment, I was at peace. Despite the niggling worry of Gran's future at Drixworths, the sun was shining; I had the people I loved with me, and life was pretty much perfect. Should have known that as soon as I'd thought it, I'd jinx it.

Jackson's ring tone blasted an obnoxious tune, shattering the silence. Wiping his hands on a rag he straightened and slid the phone out of his back pocket. My eyes followed every movement, and it occurred to me that I was thoroughly obsessed with this man.

"Ward." He answered, stretching, his muscles rippling, beckoning me. I wiped my hand across my chin in case I was drooling—the heat pooling in my belly had nothing to do with the temperature outside. Jackson listened to whoever was on the other end of the line and when his head swiveled my way, I knew it was bad news. There went our idyllic afternoon.

"On my way." Sliding the phone back in his pocket

he strode toward us, Gran sliding her sunglasses on top of her colored hair to watch him approach. Gran is never shy of her appreciation of the male form and I couldn't help but smile. She had excellent taste.

"I'm sorry, ladies," Jackson leaned down to drop a kiss on my lips, his heat radiating around me, his scent of sun, sweat, and man, intoxicating. "I've gotta go. There's been an emergency."

"But it's your day off. And Harper's birthday." Gran pouted. "Can't someone else handle it?"

He shook his head. I knew where this was going. The only reason they'd call Jackson in was if there'd been a homicide. On this beautiful sunny day, some poor unfortunate soul had died. A shiver danced across my skin.

"I'm needed on this one." He said to Gran while entwining his fingers with mine and tugging me to my feet. Cocking his head he indicated we should go inside. My stomach clenched. Was it someone I knew? Someone I called a friend? A cold, hard, sobering reality settled over me and I hurried inside, grateful for his warm hand against my lower back. In the living room, I spun to face him. "Who is it?" I asked.

"Del, one of the foxes who lives out at the compound."

I frowned. "Del? I don't think I know him." I'd been so worried it was someone I knew. "And... he's dead?" I already knew it, his nod merely confirmed it. Why else would the Whitefall Cove Police Department call him in on a day off?

Pursing his lips he nodded. "Afraid so. I'm sorry. I know I promised to work on Gran's car and then you and I could spend some quality time together..." he trailed off helplessly and I waved a hand, dismissing his apology. "Don't worry about it. I can take Gran anywhere she needs to go—you're probably doing the world a favor by keeping her off the road. Hopefully, we can still make the sunset cruise tonight."

"Agreed." He smiled then indicated his sweaty body. "Could you?"

"Sure." With a wave of my hand, my magic washed over him, transforming him from hot and disheveled to cool, clean, and crisp. Still hot, always hot, but the sweat and grease were gone, his clothes clean once more.

"Thanks, babe." Hooking an arm around my waist he pulled me against him and I cursed the fact that Del had terrible timing. What a time to die, right when I wanted to get hot and sweaty with my man.

"Hopefully, I'll be back in time for dinner." He said against my lips, and I pulled away a fraction of an inch. "I'll understand if you have to cancel."

One brow quirked in that adorable way of his. "You're sure?"

"I'll understand but it doesn't mean I have to like it." I winked. "Now go. Hurry back." I swatted his behind, and he chuckled as he headed toward the front door.

"Keep me posted," I called. As soon as the front door clicked closed behind him I headed back outside to discover Gran had stolen my deck chair and my sweet tea.

"What?" She peered at me over the top of her glasses. "You weren't here."

Shaking my head, I snatched up the towel she'd been laying on and began folding it. "That's not the point and you know it."

"Who died?" She asked, turning her attention back to her magazine, idly flicking through the pages as if she wasn't on the edge of her seat with curiosity.

"Del. A fox from the compound," I said, hugging the towel to my chest. My peaceful mood was shattered and the desire to while away the afternoon on the back deck was definitely gone. Gran's car was parked on the grass, hood up, Jackson's toolbox on the ground next to it. Using my magic, I secured the car and Jackson's tools.

"Wow. Wonder who had the balls to get the jump on a fox?" Gran said voice laced with awe. Most of the fox shifters lived in a compound on the outskirts of town and were a tight-knit community.

"We don't know how he died," I cautioned. "He could have had a heart attack."

Gran snorted. "Right. When was the last time a fox had a heart attack?"

"Okay fine. But we don't know what happened, it could be natural causes."

"Only one way to find out." I knew what the gleam in Gran's eye meant, and while common sense told me not to interfere—or investigate—I wasn't sure how long I could keep Gran from doing exactly that. And okay, I was curious myself. Plus, I didn't think Jackson would have been called in if Del had died from natural causes.

"Get changed. You're not going in that." Gran was in one of her crochet bikinis and while I loved that she was not body-conscious at all, not everyone else appreciated her eighty-year-old curves.

"Fine. Prude." She muttered under her breath, but never-the-less pulled out the wand she had tucked in the tiny band of her bikini bottoms and with a tap and a sparkle was now wearing a cute T-shirt dress. I smiled, grateful she hadn't gone with anything more revealing. "I'm going to take this lot inside and get changed myself," I told her. "Wait here."

"I don't know why you don't just use your magic, Harper!" She called after me, "it's not like you don't have an infinite supply of it, it's not going to run out if you use it you know."

I knew that. But I enjoyed doing things for myself. I was a whitelight witch, which meant I drew my magic from the stars, and it also meant I didn't need a wand to channel my powers. But that didn't mean I should use magic to do every paltry thing. It kinda felt wasteful. And lazy. I'd lived most of my life as a human, denying my witch heritage, so it felt more natural for me to do things manually rather than benefit from magic. Gran and I continued to disagree on that and probably always would.

Because Gran can't follow a simple instruction like 'wait here', she was not on the back deck when I came downstairs, face washed, a quick change from the shorts and crop top of earlier into black Capri pants and a red and white checkered blouse, the red Havaianas on my feet matching the blouse perfectly. Archie trotted behind me, his feline senses picking up the edge to my energy. I couldn't stop thinking about Del. How had he died? And why? Locking up the house I hurried to my car, shaking my head when I spotted Gran already in the passenger seat, still flicking through her magazine.

"I thought I told you to wait on the deck?" I held the door open while Archie jumped in. He eyeballed Gran who'd taken his spot, before deciding he wasn't prepared to give up his shotgun position and promptly made himself comfortable on her lap.

"Let's go. We're wasting daylight." She replied. Shaking my head, I slid behind the wheel and turned the key in the ignition.

"Just so we're clear," I said, glancing over my shoulder as I reversed out of the garage. "We're just going to take a look. We can't interfere with Jackson's investigation."

She waved a hand, "Yeah, yeah, yeah."

"Gran. Promise me."

"Did you know," she said, tossing the magazine onto the back seat and focusing her attention out the front windshield. "That honey bees can't see the color red?"

"What?" I sputtered, shoving the car into drive and heading toward the foxes compound.

"Mmmmm. Interesting, huh? Like, how did the scientists even discover that? It's not like you can just ask a bee, hey, what colors can you see?"

Mreoooow? Archie pushed his head under Gran's chin, demanding attention, and she obliged, stroking his orange fur. I then listened to a rather obscure but in-depth monologue on bees before I'd realized she'd done it to me again—distracted me with utter nonsense. Archie hung on every word Gran uttered as if he understood and I marveled at the connection she had with my familiar. Gran once told me she could understand Archie, that he spoke to her. I'd thought she'd meant in the literal sense, as in my cat spoke English, but I'd figured out it wasn't that at all—they communicated on a whole other level, whether there was a bit of telepathic magic happening or if it was just some little thing on an instinctive level, but Archie and Gran had an undeniable connection, one I'd yet to forge with my pet familiar.

The foxes compound was a hive of activity, with Jackson's car, a police vehicle, and a white van, plus a dozen or more people milling around, some in police uniform, some in white coveralls. I spied Jenna, phone out, interviewing people for her next article in the Whitefall Cove Tribune.

I pulled off the road onto the grassy verge and killed the engine, watching through the window. "There's a lot of people about," I said, more to myself than to Gran. "Wait here." Opening my door I climbed out then leaned back in. "I mean it. Do not let Archie out of this car—this is a foxes compound." And cats and foxes did not mix.

I waved to Jenna as I approached while she wrapped up her latest interview and met me halfway, greeting me with a hug. "Happy Birthday."

"Thanks," I smiled, then sobered. "What happened?"

"One of the foxes got crushed beneath his tractor. Looks like he was clearing some land, and he was on uneven terrain, the entire thing went over and he got pinned underneath."

I put a hand to my throat. "Urgh, how awful."

"Not a pleasant way to die that's for sure." She agreed.

"But the police don't suspect foul play?"

Jenna shook her head. "Not as far as I'm aware. Hey, a bit of a weird coincidence though. It was Del's birthday today too."

A shiver ran up my spine, and the hairs on my arms stood on end. Shaking it off I gave Jenna another hug then headed back to the car where Archie and Gran waited.

"Well?" Gran demanded as soon as I slid behind the wheel.

"Accidental death," I told her. "No need for the murder club to get involved."

"Darn." Gran pouted. I smirked, turned the car around, and headed back into town, confident my date with Jackson was still on, which meant I had the afternoon to myself for pampering. Coming to a halt at the front of Gran's house I kept the engine idling. She opened the door then turned to face me, her arms wrapped around Archie. "Can Archie have a sleepover?" She asked hopefully.

I blinked in surprise. "Errr, sure, don't see why not?"

"Yay!" Gran cuddled Archie a little tighter, and he bumped her chin with his head in delight.

"I'll swing by and pick him up tomorrow."

THREE

The acrid smell of sulfur seared my nostrils and for the briefest of moments, I closed my eyes. This can't be happening again, I chanted silently, over and over, but despite my deepest wish that this wasn't the case, it most assuredly was. Cracking open one eye I peered through the swirling gray cloud surrounding the creature that had appeared in front of me. I shouldn't creature shame, but holy heck, it had to be the ugliest thing I'd ever seen. It was small, with grayish almost translucent skin stretched tight over its skeletal frame, a gold ring passed through one jagged eyebrow, and beneath flared nostrils were rows and rows of spearlike teeth. Scarlet eyes flashed, and its clawed fingers and toes curled and flexed. Its eyes narrowed and those long fingers with razor-sharp talons curled before suddenly flinging out toward me.

Fight! Use your magic! My mind screamed while my heart pounded in my chest, and an icy chill swept over me. But I was too late, my reflexes too slow. A series of sharp stings hit my chest, and I looked down to see three purple darts embedded in my flesh. While I should have been running instead, I plucked out a barb and held it up, my sluggish brain processing what my eyes were seeing. *Fight!* My mind screamed again, and this time I heeded my own advice, only it was too late. It was like my body was trapped in thick molasses. Weighted. Impossible to move. I crashed to my knees, winced at the sting, knew I'd probably taken skin off. As I toppled to my side, I kept my eyes on the creature while my panicked brain tried to come up with an escape plan, but instead just went around in circles.

How could this be happening? We'd closed the rift, all the creatures that had slipped through had been banished. It was done. Finished. Over. Why then was this demon here, in my front garden, kicking my ass? My stomach roiled and the latte I'd been sipping on only moments before burned like acid in the back of my throat. Behind the vile creature was blue skies. The sun was on its descent, it would be twilight soon and I was meeting Jackson for dinner and a sunset cruise to celebrate my birthday. Upstairs hanging on the back of my bedroom door was the red dress I was planning to wear, a sexy little number I'd bought especially for the occasion. I'd run a few errands after dropping off Gran and Archie and was now ready for a couple of hours pampering.

Instead, I got this. A demon attack. In broad daylight!

I managed to shoot off a spark of magic, but it missed the demon and bounced off the side of the lighthouse cottage I called home. The demon snickered, gestured as if to say come get me. I tried to push myself upright, but all I managed to do was push myself in a semi-circle on the ground. The demon cackled some more and the stench of sulfur became stronger while I struggled not to gag. My heart slammed into my throat. I was powerless. Vulnerable. With no close neighbors, there was no-one to help, no-one to see, no-one to save me. *Save yourself!* My inner voice was becoming a real pain but nevertheless, I began to drag myself across the ground, making slow progress. I could taste it in the air. Dead. Stale. It was choking and rank and I wanted to vomit. I could feel its red eyes on me as it snaked closer, closing the gap between us, could only watch as vapor swirled and gathered into a thick suffocating smoke.

A loud KABOOM shattered the eerie silence that had settled over us. The demon screeched, flying backward through the air, a gaping hole in its chest that I could see clear through. Laying on the ground I watched as its body shriveled and hissed, before exploding into a million flecks of light.

A pair of feet appeared by my head. "You okay?" Annie Robins, head witch of the Sisters of the Sacred Flame Coven asked.

"Ack." I garbled, my throat constricted. I was running out of time, whatever the little bastard had dosed those darts with was working. That's why it hadn't finished me off. It had been content to watch and taunt, because it knew its poison was already pumping through my veins, bringing about my end.

"Relax. You're not dying." Annie said. Squinting I watched as she came into view, wand dangling from her hand. "This is gonna sting." She held up what had to be the biggest metal syringe in the entire world. I wanted to scream *wait!* but she slammed it down into my thigh and pressed the plunger. My eyes rolled into the back of my head as whatever was in the syringe burned a path through my body. My back arched off the ground, my breath caught in my throat, and every hair on my body stood on end as I thrummed with electricity. And then it was over. I collapsed back onto the dirt with an exhaled wheeze.

"I'm glad my spidey senses were right." She said conversationally, crouched by my side, idly plucking the barbs out of my chest. "Something told me you were in trouble, glad I got here in time. Oh, and that was a Garrag." She dropped the barbs into a ziplock bag and tossed them into a canvas bag on the ground by her side.

"A what?" My voice came out like I'd been on a three-day bender at a seedy bar. Rusty as old nails. I cleared my throat and tried again. "A what?"

"Garrag." She repeated, standing and slinging the bag over one shoulder. She was dressed in blue jeans, and a floral shirt, sandals on her feet. She looked like a sweet seventy-year-old lady, not the badass witch who'd just saved my butt. Now that I had my wits about me I noticed the car pulled up by my front gate. I hadn't even heard her arrive.

"A lesser demon, but still," she shrugged one shoulder, her voice trailing off.

"A lesser demon..." I echoed. Annie was examining the lighthouse cottage, hands on hips, feet planted. She gave off a vibe of someone in total control, that battling a demon wasn't anything to be concerned about. Unlike myself who was a wobbly mess sitting on the ground. A wet nose suddenly nuzzled into my neck and I let out a scream, jerking backward. Next to me Annie's dalmatian, Rupert, stood, tail wagging, his entire body shaking with enthusiasm.

"Easy Rupert," Annie said without turning around.

I let out a relieved chuckle. "Hey, Rupert." I patted the dog's head, and he immediately crawled onto my lap, only Rupert didn't seem to realize he was not lap dog size, with limbs and elbows digging into me as he tried to get comfortable. Annie snapped her fingers, and Rupert immediately abandoned me to trot to her side. "Search." She told him. Off he went nose to the ground.

"What's he searching for?" I asked, gingerly clambering to my feet. Everything dipped and swayed for a moment and I held still, gulping in great gasps of air. Annie shot me a look over her shoulder that I couldn't decipher.

"Mushrooms." She said.

"Really?" I couldn't keep the surprise out of my voice.

She snorted as if I was a moron. "No! Demons!" Oh. That made more sense.

"Is that how you knew the Garrag was here? Because Rupert could smell it?"

Annie heaved a sigh as if her patience was wearing thin. Maybe it was. "I picked it up on my radar."

"You have a demon radar?"

She folded her arms and considered me. "It's time we had a talk, Harper."

"Oh?" I squeaked. This didn't sound good.

"Alice convinced me to let her take the lead with your training when you returned to Whitefall Cove and rejoined the coven. I'm starting to see that wasn't the wisest of moves."

I blinked in surprise. Where was this coming from?

I'd taken the required refresher course from Drixworths when my witches' license had been temporarily suspended. I'd sat—and passed—my witches exam. It was news to me that the coven was unhappy with me. Worry churned in my gut. Were they going to kick me out?

She gave a brief nod then headed toward my cottage. "At least the wards are still in place."

Hurrying after her I asked, "have I done something wrong?"

She stopped so suddenly I nearly ran into her. "Wrong?" She laughed then, the sound so different to her voice that I was momentarily taken aback. Her laugh was... magical. Soft and melodic, at total odds with the slightly grating harshness of her voice. Why had I never noticed that about Annie before? I frowned. Surely I'd heard Annie laugh before... hadn't I?

"I have then," I muttered more to myself than to her, but she heard me and responded, anyway. "Define "wrong"." Then I began walking again, climbing the three stairs to my front deck and waiting for me to catch up. I hurried after her, unlocked the front door and pushed it open before somewhat cautiously stepping over the threshold. If a demon had been waiting for me outside, what's to say something worse wasn't waiting inside? *Oh duh. The wards!* I really was off my game.

Annie followed me inside, her eyes giving the room a once over before coming to rest on me. "You might be a whitelight witch, but you're weak." She said. I reared back as if she'd slapped me. *Weak?* That wasn't right. I was a powerful witch, everyone told me so. I crossed my arms and frowned at her. "I'm not," I argued, affronted that she'd called me weak, of all things.

She snorted. "You are. That Garrag shouldn't have been a problem for you. You could have dispatched it with a snap of your fingers. Why didn't you?"

Damn it, she had me. "I was getting to it." I harrumphed, not enjoying being on the back foot.

"Right." She nodded, a smirk curving one corner of her mouth. "So if I hadn't intervened you'd have taken care of it?"

"Eventually." I lied.

She saw right through my false bravado and burst into peals of laughter. "You're priceless!" She chortled. I shifted uncomfortably, not used to being at the pointy end of someone's derision, and I have to say, not a fan. Seconds ticked by while I waited for Annie to get her mirth under control. Eventually, she did, wiping her fingers beneath her eyes.

"We're going to have a problem if you're not prepared to use your magic." It was a statement, not a question.

"I use it!" Keen to change the subject I headed for the fridge and pulled out a bottle of wine and poured myself a hefty glass. After downing the contents in one gulp, I refilled the glass. "Wine?" I offered belatedly.

Annie was watching me with her green eyes, judging, probably labeling me an alcoholic on top of being a weak witch. Color me surprised when she nodded and said, "sure."

FOUR

Sitting opposite Annie at my kitchen table, I watched as she wrapped her fingers around the wineglass, the silver skull ring she wore on her middle finger clinking against the glass as she lifted it to her lips.

"So what brings you here today?" I asked, feeling more in control now that I'd had a shot of alcohol to fortify me.

"I told you. I had a sense you were in trouble. Plus, you and I are long overdue for a chat."

I swallowed. "Oh?"

"Harper, your Gran assured me when you rejoined the coven that you were absolutely, positively, one hundred percent, in."

I nodded. "I am."

"Explain to me then, why you've ditched the last three coven meets?"

Three? I'd missed three? No wonder she was mad. While I madly scrambled through my memories as to why I hadn't attended, she continued. "You've turned your back on the sisterhood before. Turned your back on your magic and lived your life as a human." She held up a hand to silence me when I would have interrupted. "I have no argument with that. You do what you have to do. But witches in my coven? They are witches. We are family. We don't have one foot in, one foot out. If you have even the slightest of doubts, then the Sisters of the Sacred Flame are not for you."

I sucked in a shocked breath. I'd had no idea Annie felt this way. The mere thought that she'd kick me out rattled me.

"I'm sorry." I was. "I'll try harder." And I would.

"Good. Oh, and happy birthday."

"Thank you." I took another sip of my wine, felt the effects of it hit my system, warming my blood, and making my head spin. I put the glass down. I didn't want to be totally wasted for my date with Jackson tonight. Which reminded me, I needed to get ready. I'd already lost some pampering time thanks to my tussle with the Garrag but all was not lost, there was still time to shower and do my hair and makeup. I eyed Annie, wondering if it would be rude to ask her to leave. We'd cleared the air, she'd saved my butt and delivered her warning about me skipping coven meetings.

Annie's eyes landed on the small box sitting in the middle of the table, the yellow ribbon that had been neatly tied around it now unraveled around the base. I watched, puzzled, while Annie held her hand over the box and closed her eyes. Seconds passed before her eyes snapped open and pinned me to my seat.

"What's in the box?" She asked. Before I could answer she pushed back her chair and headed to the front door. I sagged in relief. She was leaving. Good. I could get on with my evening plans in peace. I stood and made my way to the stairs, freezing with one foot on the bottom step when the front door opened again. I slowly glanced over my shoulder. It was Annie, carrying the canvas bag she'd left outside.

Shoulders slumping I swiveled and rejoined her back at the dining table.

"I asked," she said, "what's in the box?"

I lifted my shoulders. "A birthday present."

"From?"

"There wasn't a card. I assume from one of my friends. It was on my doorstep when I got up this morning."

She paused in rummaging in her bag to shoot me a look. "If it was from a friend wouldn't they have given it to you in person?"

"Well... yeah, I guess so." In all honesty, I hadn't given it much thought.

"How old are you now?"

"Thirty-three."

She nodded once then produced a set of metal tongs and began easing the lid off the box.

"What are you doing?" I protested, moving to pick up the box. She held up a hand. "Stop! Don't touch it." The authority and conviction in her voice had me freezing in place.

"What?" I protested. "It's fine. It's just an old medallion."

Annie shook her head and continued to lift the lid off the box. As soon as it slid free, she placed it to one side, her movements slow and deliberate as if diffusing a bomb. She glanced at the medallion nestled on a bed of yellow silk. I stole a peek. It looked exactly as it had this morning when I'd opened the box. A rusty old relic, innocuous, harmless. I'd been running late, so I'd slid the lid back on and left it on the table and hadn't spared it another thought all day.

"What is it?" I whispered, starting to feel worried that I'd brought something dangerous into my home.

"What you have here is an Astrudian Amulet," Annie replied, pulling a rock from her bag. I watched, fascinated, as she clasped the rock between her hands and twisted. It opened to reveal a hollowed-out middle.

"A rock trinket box," I said under my breath. She ignored me, picking up the tongs and clasping the amulet, she dropped it into the hollowed-out stone, placed the top back on, and twisted it closed. Then she tossed the rock in the air, caught it in one hand with a grin, and lobbed it into her bag.

"Taken care of." She said, dusting her hands together.

"What is an A-whatever Amulet?" I asked, chewing my lip.

"An Astrudian Amulet is a relic," she replied, zipping the bag closed. "From between worlds. The question is, what is an Astrudian Amulet doing here?"

"Here? In my house?" I asked. I'd never heard of an Astrudian Amulet and made a mental note to check some ancient books in the bookstore to investigate further. I wondered who had left the amulet for me and wondered why they hadn't knocked on the door and delivered the gift in person.

"Here, in this realm."

I froze. "So when you say, between worlds... you mean... another realm?" I had flashbacks of the rift and our town being flooded with creatures from another dimension.

"Astrudian Amulets are currency for crossroads demons." She explained, watching me with arms crossed over her chest. "Know any of those?"

"What! Me?" I squeaked, "No!"

"And yet here you are, in possession of one."

"I told you," I protested. "I found it on my doorstep this morning. It's a birthday gift."

Annie snorted. "Some gift. Whoever left it sure doesn't like you much."

"You're saying it's a bad thing? You didn't touch it with your hands," I narrowed my eyes. "Why?" My mind was going over every conceivable answer and not liking anything that my overactive imagination came up with, from my hands melting off to turning into a demon at one touch.

"Touching an Astrudian Amulet will mark your soul."

"As having made a deal with a crossroads demon? The crossroads demon where you make a deal with the devil? Where you bargain your soul?"

Annie nodded. "The very same."

"What does that even mean?" I needed to know what was going on, especially if someone had targeted me with this gift.

"You know crossroads demons are the demon you summon—at a crossroads—for some deal that would benefit you, in exchange for your soul. That soul would be collected at an agreed-upon time in the future. It depends on your negotiating skills how much time you have before you die and your soul goes to hell. Could be one year, could be ten."

"Yes." I nodded. "That's how I understand it. How

do the Astrudian Amulets play into it? You said currency?"

"It allows a crossroads demon to reap your soul with no deal in place."

I sucked in a horrified breath. Someone had gifted me a medallion—a coin— that would cost me my soul. I felt heat wash over me, sweat beading my brow. I'd been so close to death and didn't even realize it.

"That hardly seems fair," I complained. "I don't want to make a deal with a crossroads demon. And I don't want the coin." I harrumphed.

"Good thing you didn't touch it then." She smirked. "The shuntis rock blocks the coins' magic."

"But why me? And why now?" I was struggling to believe someone disliked me so much they'd do such a thing. I don't have a big enough ego to think every one loved me, but I didn't think anyone hated me enough to want me dead.

"The coins are more powerful on a person's day of birth."

What a perfect way to get the coin into my possession on my birthday. Disguise it as a gift. And I'd fallen for it. If it weren't for Annie, I could have potentially lost my soul to a crossroads demon. Seems she'd saved me twice today.

"How do you know all of this?" I asked, sinking on to a chair.

"It's what I do. I'm a witch. I take my heritage

seriously." She picked up the bag and slung it over one shoulder. "Remind me, who else has a birthday today?"

A shiver ran up my spine. Oh no. The fox shifter, Del! Jenna had said it was his birthday today. Had he received a coin? Had he touched it and that's why he'd died because the crossroads demon had reaped his soul while he'd been driving his tractor?

"What is it?" Annie was watching the flurry of emotions cross my face.

"There was a death today," I explained. "A fox shifter who I didn't know, but someone told me today was his birthday too."

"Damn." Annie cursed hands on hips. "That's unfortunate. Anyone else?"

I ran a hand through my hair, trying to think. "Tiny. She runs Tiny's Garage. Do you think the demon has delivered a coin to her too?"

"It probably wasn't the demon. This stinks of a demon deal though—this could be the trade someone has done, saving their own soul in exchange for someone else's. The demon doesn't care, a soul is a soul."

"So the demon would have given that person the coins?"

"Possibly. But the coins could have come from anywhere. We also have to acknowledge that whoever had this coin may not have known its origins, didn't know what it would do."

"But they could hardly be innocent because they'd have had to touch the coin. And if they'd done that, it would mark their own soul."

"Unless the crossroads demon gave them immunity." She said.

Tension was giving me a headache and all my excitement for tonight's celebrations with Jackson had all but disappeared. My phone rang, startling me. Glancing at the screen I saw it was Gran and frowned. I hoped she hadn't had trouble with Garrags as well.

"Harper! We've got trouble, or more importantly, you've got trouble."

Oh my God, how did she know? Did she pick it up through the witches' grapevine or something? "It's okay Gran," I assured her. "I know about the Garrag."

"Pft, a Garrag is nothing."

I hung my head, wondering how much worse this could get. So much for my peaceful, relaxing birthday. I felt like I'd gone from zero to one hundred in three seconds flat.

"It's Archie," Gran told me, and my heart stopped in my chest.

"What's happened?" I cried, frantically searching around for my keys.

"I think he ate a sprite," Gran said. I froze. Seconds

ticked by. "What?" I croaked, my heart finally resuming as relief washed over me. Unless sprites were toxic to cats, then we had a problem.

"A sprite has been hanging out in my lemon tree lately and I let Archie out to do his business and when he came back in he was licking his lips and I swear his belly is rounder."

"Are you sure he... ate it?"

"Well... no." She admitted.

"You speak cat, why not just ask him?" I pointed out.

"I think he knows he'd be in trouble if he did, so he's not talking." I almost laughed out loud. Smart cat.

"Okay, well, have you checked outside? To see if the sprite is still in the tree?" I suggested, crossing my fingers it was, and that this was one crisis we'd manage to avert on my birthday.

"Excellent idea." I listened as Gran opened the back door and stepped outside, heard her footsteps crunch on the gravel, knew the precise moment the gravel gave way to lawn. Then. "Oh! There you are!" She cried in delight.

"I take it you've spotted the sprite?" I drawled.

"Yes. Seems Archie didn't eat it after all."

"Well, I have trained him not to hunt the wildlife," I replied, "so I'd have been very surprised if he'd actually eaten it." Turning my back on Annie I headed into the kitchen, debating what to tell Gran about Annie's visit and the coin.

I'd had a feeling, ever since the rift was opened and supernatural creatures from another dimension invaded Whitefall Cove, that something was coming for me. Llewellyn the demon hunter had been the one to tell me I was a whitelight witch, meaning I drew my power from the stars, rather than the earth. Turns out whitelight witches are rare. And having unique magic puts a bullseye on one's back. But after the rift had been closed, and the creatures banished, life had settled back into its normal pattern and I'd relaxed, let my guard down.

Until today. A Garrag—a creature I'd never even heard of before—had attacked. And then Annie had turned up and stopped me from touching an Astrudian Amulet that would have marked my soul for a crossroads demon to take. I glanced at her now, stunned to discover she was no longer sitting at the table.

Frowning I scanned the living room. No sign of her.

"Hang on a sec, Gran," I said into the phone, then ran upstairs. Maybe Annie had needed to use the bathroom. Only she wasn't upstairs. I flew back downstairs, flung open the front door, and spied Annie leaning against her car, arms crossed, face tilted up to the sun. How did she leave the house without making a sound?

"Harper, you there?" Gran's voice was tinny in my ear and I turned my attention back to the call.

"Gran, when I came back to Whitefall Cove and rejoined the coven, did Annie have an issue with that?" I asked, curious about what Annie had told me earlier.

"What?" Gran barked, "Not that I know of. She did say you'd turned your back on magic for a long time and someone needed to keep an eye on you."

"And you volunteered?"

"You know, now that you mention it, Annie didn't seem to think that was a good idea. But I insisted. You're my granddaughter, of course I should take you under my wing and help you re-learn your magic."

Rupert came trotting out of the sand dunes, tail in the air. Annie pushed away from her car and whistled. Rupert changed course and headed toward her, joy in every bouncing step. He was such a cutie. Annie opened the rear door and Rupert jumped inside. "You coming?" She called to me. Holding my hand over the phone I called back, "where?"

"Tiny's Garage."

A shiver danced over my skin. Del shared a birthday with me, and now he was dead. Tiny also shared a birthday with me. Was Annie's hunch correct and Tiny had been given a coin as well? I couldn't risk it. "Gran, I've got to go. I'll talk to you later." I disconnected the call. "I'll take my own car!" I called out to Annie. I saw the flash of white teeth as she smiled and thought I saw her mouth the word "chicken". Rushing back into the house I snatched up my keys and locked up behind me, placing my hand on the ward by the front door to strengthen it. But that hadn't helped with the coin. I'd brought it into the house voluntarily and that rattled me more than I cared to admit.

Keeping one eye on the road and one on my rearview mirror, I headed back into town, Annie following. Most of the businesses on Main Street were now closed and the clock on the dash told me it had just turned six o'clock. Still time to make my date with Jackson if I hurried. He'd texted me to say dinner was still on, that Del's case was open and shut. I could check on Tiny and once I knew she was okay, that would leave me with enough time to shower and dress. I wouldn't get the bubble bath I'd been looking forward to, nor the face mask Jenna had given me for my birthday.

Driving into the parking lot I eyed the garage. One roller door was fully closed, the other rolled down partway, leaving a two-foot gap at the bottom. Lights shone from inside, and I could hear the radio blaring. Annie pulled in next to me, her car rumbling and vibrating the earth under my feet. I waited at the trunk of my car while she let Rupert out. He immediately jumped down and headed toward the garage, nose sniffing the ground as he went.

"Ummmmm." I wasn't sure how Tiny would feel about a dog in her garage and I had visions of her lobbing a spanner at the unsuspecting hound.

"What's up?" Annie asked.

"About Tiny..." I chewed my lip. "She can be a bit... difficult." That was putting it mildly.

"I can handle difficult," Annie assured me and stepped toward the garage. That's when Rupert kicked off, his bark frantic. Annie took off at a run, shouting over her shoulder, "stay there!"

Of course, I didn't. I followed, keeping my eyes on the garage door where Rupert stood barking at whoever was inside. I assumed it was Tiny and was expecting to hear the sounds of world war three erupting any minute. The fairy would not be happy about this intrusion into her garage. Annie reached the roller door and deftly ducked beneath it, snapping her fingers at Rupert, who immediately lapsed into silence. I jogged up to the door, puffing. I really needed to get fit, I told myself. I tried to execute the same smooth maneuver Annie had done when she'd crouched under the roller door, instead, I overbalanced and ended up on my hands and knees, crawling beneath the door instead. Standing on the other side I brushed myself off, apologized to my already bruised knees for the rough treatment they'd received today, then glanced around.

"Oh my God!" I squeaked.

"You might want to look away if you're squeamish," Annie said. I swallowed the bile in my throat. Too late. Tiny was crushed beneath the yellow car she'd been working on earlier today. Her upper body lay in a pool of blood, her lifeless face staring up at the ceiling, while her lower body was trapped beneath the car. I sucked in a deep breath, only that accentuated the coppery scent of blood in the air and made my stomach churn.

"Accident?" I croaked, eyes darting around the workshop. It all seemed so innocuous, so mundane. The radio still played, the scent of oil fought with the scent of Tiny's blood. The garage itself was a mess, but that was Tiny's way. Among the chaos and haphazardly stacked shelves and benches, she could lay her hands on what she needed when she needed it.

"I guess the hoist could have failed," Annie said, walking the length of the car. I could see now that it was sitting on a hoist, one of those ones where the mechanic could walk underneath, and Tiny was trapped beneath it. Another wave of nausea churned in my stomach when I pictured the car falling. Tiny didn't stand a chance. Annie walked all the way around the car then came to squat by Tiny.

"Interesting." She murmured, more to herself than to me.

"What is it?" I whispered, having no idea why I was whispering.

"She has a mark on her forehead, see?" Annie pointed and I peered closer at Tiny's face. Sure enough, there was a red scrape on her forehead, just above her right eyebrow. "Yet she's fallen backward. How did she get that graze?"

"She could have bumped her head while working under the car?" I pointed out, remembering she'd done exactly that when I'd dropped into the garage this morning.

"Possibly. But she's a fairy. Any bumps and skinned knuckles would heal fast. Plus, she's an experienced mechanic, yes? And she'd probably be more aware than most—due to her size—of her spatial requirements. You'd expect mechanics to have skinned knuckles from slipped spanners. Not bumps on the head."

I ran my fingers through my hair. I had no idea. Maybe Tiny hit her head a lot, maybe she didn't. She was a fairy; they healed quickly. Only this bump hadn't healed because she'd died.

"Search for an Astrudian Amulet," Annie ordered.

"What? We need to call the police." I protested.

"And we will. Once we've found the amulet."

My mouth dropped open. "You think that's what caused this? That Tiny received a crossroads demon's coin and then... died?"

"Possibly." Annie rubbed her chin. "Can't rule it out."

"Is that how these Astrudian Amulet's work?" I cried, "You get given one, and then you're killed!" I must have misunderstood what Annie had told me earlier about the amulets—or demon coins as I thought of them. I'd figured if you touched one it marked you. That you still had time. But if Tiny had been given a coin today, on her birthday, and now she was dead? And Del, the fox? Had he received a coin? It made my own experience that much scarier. I would be dead now if not for Annie!

"Calm down," Annie began poking around on a bench at the back of the garage. "We need to find the amulet and take it into safekeeping before someone else gets their hands on it."

"We need to call the police." I protested, pulling out my phone. Annie was by my side in an instant, fingers tight around my wrist. "Are you sure you want to do that?" Her husky voice held a hint of menace.

"Call the authorities?" I snapped, tugging my wrist free from her grasp. "Yes! There's been a murder."

"A murder that's been staged to look like an accident." Annie pointed out. I chanced a quick look in Tiny's direction. Annie was right. This looked like an accident—the police would most likely think it was one too, and while I was confident Jackson would believe me when I told him about the amulets and what we believed had happened, we had no evidence, no proof. I chewed my lip, considering my options. If I called the police, the garage would become a crime scene. If I held off, we'd have the chance to look around and search for clues, find out who did this to Tiny.

"Fine. Ten minutes, then I'm calling."

Annie grinned then snapped her fingers. Rupert,

who'd been lying in the opening of the roller door, jumped to his feet and trotted to her side. She crouched on one knee and ruffled his fur. His tail swept the floor in a perfect arc. "I know you can feel it, boy," she whispered. "I can feel it too."

"Feel what?" I butted in.

"Demon." She glanced at me, rubbing her cheek against Rupert's. "But it's odd. I can feel their energy, but it's not strong. It's almost as if someone else has come into contact with a demon and that energy has attached to them."

"So... you think Tiny...?" I trailed off, my mind a whirl. Tiny had a colorful past. She'd been the head mechanic for one of the top car racing teams in the country, had toured the circuit and really made a name for herself. Then the team had started losing, and they'd blamed Tiny, firing her. She'd come home to Whitefall Cove, bought the garage, and that was that, no more car racing. I wondered now if her success all those years ago was because of a deal with a crossroads demon? And today was collection day?

"It's fun watching you think." Annie drawled, still embracing her dog. "But no. This—" she waved at Tiny's body, "is not how a crossroads demon would reap your soul."

"How then?"

She cocked her head, then between one blink and the next she was in front of me. I staggered back in surprise. For an old girl, she was incredibly nimble on her feet. "Your soul leaving your body doesn't have to be violent," she said. "If I were to reap your soul right now? Your mortal body would simply crumple to the floor. The host doesn't have to be killed to get the soul, the soul is simply... taken." She snapped her fingers, and I shivered. I backed up a step. Annie followed. For a little thing, she sure was intimidating. I swallowed the lump in my throat. "You can reap souls?" It came out on a squeak and I cleared my throat, "You can reap souls?" I repeated. I was seeing a side to the head witch of my coven I'd never seen before and I didn't know what to make of it.

She studied me for a moment, her green eyes intense, almost hypnotizing. Then she threw back her head and laughed. "No."

My shoulders sagged. She'd had me going for a minute.

"But I don't think this is the work of a demon deal." She crossed her arms over her chest and studied Tiny's body.

"Why not?" It sounded plausible to me.

"Because I can only sense a faint trace of a demon. If one had been here, claiming his prize, I'd know. And Rupert would know. As it is, he's on edge, but no demon has been here... at least not recently."

"So you're saying this isn't related to the Astrudian Amulet?"

She shook her head. "I don't believe so. But we should search the place, just in case. But Tiny's death? Not related. She was murdered plain and simple."

I snorted. Nothing plain and simple about being murdered. Sliding my phone back into my pocket I gave a brief nod. "Fine. We won't call the cops—yet." I wasn't one hundred percent buying Annie's theory.

"Go search the office," Annie instructed. "I'll take care of the workshop."

I bristled, tiring of being bossed around by the diminutive witch. "Why? Why don't you take the office and I'll do out here?"

She sighed. "Because watching you think is giving me a headache. You're trying to decide if you believe me or not. Fine. Whatever, I don't care. But we've got limited time and you move slower than molasses. I move faster. The office is smaller. By the time you're done in there, I'll be done out here."

"Fine." I snapped, offended that she'd called me slow. But she did have a point. She moved fast. Real fast. So I guess in comparison I moved slow. But that was two insults in one day, and I'd like to think I had a thicker skin, but it rankled. Slow and weak. Not two words I'd use to describe myself. Stomping across the workshop floor I headed toward the door marked office and flung it open. A voice screeched "Don't touch that!" and I nearly peed my pants in fright, quickly slamming the door closed.

Rupert jumped to his feet and barked up a storm while Annie rolled her shoulders and headed toward me. "Rupert, shush." She said. The dog immediately quieted but trotted by her heels, his nose sniffing and snuffling at the bottom of the door.

"Someone is in there," I whispered, hand on my chest. Why hadn't they come out earlier? Surely they'd have heard the hoist failing and the car crashing to the floor? Not to mention Annie and I talking. Was it the murderer? Hiding in the office until we left? But that was a stupid plan, for surely they'd realize we'd call the cops—they had no hope of getting out of the office undetected.

"Would you just stop thinking!" Annie groaned. "It's exhausting, and I wasn't lying earlier, you're giving me a headache." Then she put her hand on the doorknob and twisted. "I'll take care of this." She said, before slipping inside and closing the door firmly behind her. I pressed my ear up against the wood and listened, heard whoever was inside say "don't touch that!" again.

"What's going on?" A voice said from behind me.

My heart leaped into my throat and I'm pretty sure this time I did pee, just a little. Hand to my chest I spun around to find Gran standing there. Even Rupert was taken by surprise, emitting a little yip before turning his attention to Gran and giving her a thorough sniffing before licking her hand.

"Hey, boy." Gran cooed, getting to her knees and wrapping her arms around Rupert who accepted her affection with gusto, his tail doing double time. In between face licks Gran glanced at me. "Well, Harper? What's going on? And why did you kill Tiny?"

"What?" I blinked. "I didn't kill her!" I protested. "And how did you know I was here?"

"Location spell." Gran finally released Rupert and got back to her feet. I shook my head, typical witches never could mind their own business. I ignored the fact that I was snooping through a dead woman's garage.

I eyeballed Gran from head to toe. "What are you wearing?"

"What, this? I had a feeling you were up to no good, so I dressed accordingly." She was all in black. Black leggings, a black hoodie, black runners. The runners were a surprise. Usually, Gran got around in bedazzled Ugg boots. Right now she looked like a cat burglar.

"You definitely look like you're up to no good." I sighed. But I didn't have any ground to stand on myself.

"So what's the story?" Gran asked. No matter how much I wanted to keep Gran out of it, keeping her out of anything was nigh on impossible. And something told me that there was more to Annie's concerns over me than either witch was saying.

SEVEN

The door to the office opened and Annie reappeared, the ugliest bird I'd ever seen perched on her wrist. It was bald. And green. It had massive feet and a round belly. "Don't touch that!" It squawked.

Gran, who apparently wasn't concerned with the fact that there was a dead body behind her was one hundred percent focused on Annie and the bird. With a small jump of excitement, punctuated with a fart, she stepped toward Annie, hands outstretched.

"Oh, come here you poor baby." She cooed, holding out her arm. The bird eyeballed her from head to toe, head cocked as if considering if she could be trusted or not. He gave a brief nod which is when I noticed a strip of brown feathers poking out the top of his head like a mohawk. He shuffled his way along Annie's hand and transferred himself over to Gran's.

"What's your name?" Gran asked him.

"Don't touch that!" He squawked. I snorted. Figured he repeated what he heard the most—Tiny yelling at him not to touch something. Gran lifted her other hand and stroked down his back and he gave a little wriggle of delight, his knobby knees bending up and down as he did a happy dance. Gran looked over at me, a wide smile on her face. "He's gorgeous."

"He really isn't," I argued. He was seriously the ugliest bird I'd ever seen.

"Shh." Gran soothed the bird. "Don't listen to her." She turned her back and that's when I noticed the bird had a total of three red feathers sticking out its butt. Bald if not for his mohawk and tail feathers. Trust Gran to fall head over heels for it.

"What are you doing here, Alice?" Annie planted her hands on her hips and nodded toward Gran who'd moved several feet away and was cooing at the bird.

"Came to see what Harper was up to," Gran replied without looking up from the bird.

"Did you call her?" Annie asked me. Shaking my head, I said, "absolutely not. The least people involved the better."

"You here to find out who squished Tiny?" Gran asked. "Wasn't you was it?" She added, narrowing her eyes.

"Wasn't me," Annie confirmed, not taken aback in the slightest that Gran had just insinuated that the leader of our coven may also be a murderer. "But your Granddaughter was gifted an Astrudian Amulet for her birthday—and since she and Tiny share a birthday I figured it best if we checked in on her. Unfortunately, we were too late."

"A devil coin?" Gran gasped.

"You know of them?" Annie asked.

Gran nodded. "I've heard of them. Never seen one aside from a picture in a book."

Inclining her head Annie turned her attention away from Gran and back to Tiny's garage. "We were about to search the garage, see if Tiny has an amulet."

"You think a demon did this?" Gran was asking all the questions I'd asked. Annie repeated her answers. "No, I don't. I think this–" she waved a hand at Tiny's body, "was murder. Harper is keen to call the authorities but before we do that, I want to make certain there is no amulet here." She swiveled on her heel and resumed her search, Rupert joining her to snuffle among the boxes and discarded rags on the floor. Gran moved closer to me and stage whispered, "You didn't touch that amulet did you?"

"No," I whispered back. "And why are we whispering?"

Gran blinked, then grinned. "Oh. Right. I dunno, so as not to disturb the dead I guess?" I couldn't contain a chuckle. "I'm sure Tiny won't mind. If she was murdered, who better than us to solve it?"

Gran busted out a dance move, the bird on her arm joining in. "The murder club is back in business," she chortled.

"Annie's right though," I warned. "We're going to have to call the police. So before we do that, now's our chance to have a look around."

Gran nodded. "To search for clues."

"And an Astrudian Amulet." Annie reminded us.

"Yes, and the amulet," I agreed. "Gran, why don't you help Annie out here, and I'll do the office?"

The office was like the workshop. A disaster. An enormous desk dominated the room with papers, flyers, and oily rags littering the surface. A rusty green filing cabinet was jammed behind the door, all the drawers partially open and from what I could see the files inside were packed in so tight they were overflowing. The cracked window was covered in wire mesh and in front of it stood a perch. By the mountain of bird poop on the floor beneath it I assumed this was where Tiny's bird spent most of its time. Hefting a phone book off the top of the filing cabinet I used it to prop the door open to relieve some of the stench.

"Where do I start?" I whispered to myself, surveying the room. So far no sign of a gift box like the one left on my doorstep. In fact, there was no sign that anyone had remembered today was Tiny's birthday at all. No flowers, no cards. Gingerly I eased myself into the cracked leather seat behind her desk and using the hem of my shirt, I pulled open the top drawer. No gift box, nor amulet, but there was a cash box. Grabbing a dirty rag of the desk I used it to lift the cash box out of the drawer, not wanting to leave my fingerprints behind.

"God, Tiny, ever heard of locks?" I muttered, flicking the lid open. My mouth dropped open at the amount of cash inside. There had to be thousands! On top of it was a scribbled note with some numbers and dollar amounts. Grabbing my phone I snapped a photo of the note before closing the lid and shoving the cash box back into the drawer. I quickly searched the rest of the desk, no sign of a gift box or amulet, but I saw a couple of invoices that had been torn out of a pre-printed book—the numbers matched what was written on the note in the cash tin.

"One twenty-nine." I read aloud. "A two hundred and fifty dollar deposit paid by one Jodie Bell." I snapped a photo, then read the other invoice. "One one ten. Glen Weaver. Eighty dollars."

"How's it going in here?" Annie asked from the doorway.

"No sign of an amulet," I replied absently, my mind occupied with the mystery of why Tiny was keeping so much cash on her premises—in a cash tin that wasn't locked. In a drawer that wasn't locked. In an office that wasn't locked. "Is there a safe in here?" I wondered out loud, pushing the chair back I checked behind the calendar that hung lopsided on the wall, then the floor, lifting the threadbare rug that sat beneath Tiny's desk.

"Why is a safe important? You think she would have put the amulet in there?" Annie stepped forward, but I was shaking my head. "No, not at all. Tiny doesn't appear to be the type to put anything away. If she was given an amulet as a gift like I was, it would most likely be sitting right here on her desk, or on a shelf out in her workshop. She'd have probably just put it down on the nearest available surface."

"Why are you interested in a safe then?"

I leaned forward, resting my elbows on the edge of the desk. "I'm just curious. She has an unlocked cash box in her drawer. I would assume she'd lock it up. Oh, unless she took it home with her each night!" That probably made more sense. Tiny was a successful businesswoman, and while her garage was messy, she had a system. I could picture her in my mind's eye tucking the cash box under her arm, grabbing the invoice book with it, and taking it home with her each night to reconcile the payments she'd received that day. That's why she'd scribbled down the invoice numbers and dollar amounts on a scrap of paper—she had every intention of updating her records later.

"I think Tiny does some of her paperwork at home," I said to Annie.

"She still lives across the road?"

"Yep. Right there." I pointed to Tiny's house, directly across the street from the garage.

"And she still lives alone?"

"Yes, as far as I know."

Annie gave a slight nod. "Right. I'm done here. I will swing by and check out Tiny's house, then I'm out of here." She dusted her hands together and spun on her heel, quickly leaving the office. "Rupert! Come!" I heard her call.

"Wait!" I shouted, hurrying after her. "You're leaving?"

She'd paused at the roller door. "I've done what I came to do."

"But what about the authorities?"

"What about them?"

"Well, they'll want to talk to you." I blustered, surprised that she'd leave before the police had arrived. Rather than answer me she quirked one gray brow, then ducked beneath the roller door, disappearing from view. Seconds later I heard the roar of her car.

"Shit," I whispered, surprised that she'd left.

"What is it, hun?" Gran sidled up to me, stroking the almost featherless bird perched on her arm.

"Annie has gone," I said.

"So?"

"So? I'm about to call the police that Tiny is dead. Annie is a witness. We are too. She shouldn't have left." I grumbled, pulling out my phone and jabbing at the screen. Now I was going to have to explain everything on my own—I don't know why it rattled me so much that Annie had done a runner, but it did. Although she had said she was going to Tiny's house, I could direct the police there.

Jackson answered on the second ring, "Hey babe, looking forward to that lobster tonight?"

Darn. Our date had slipped my mind, what with finding Tiny dead on her garage floor. "Yeah... about that." I sighed.

"What's happened?" His tone held just a hit of concern and a butt load of resignation. I didn't blame him. Between the two of us we'd had to cancel our last two dates, and I'd been looking forward to celebrating my birthday with him. But this one wasn't my fault. A murder trumped dinner any day of the week and despite Jackson being due to knock off any minute, it would be him canceling this time, not me. I pushed down the annoying little voice that reminded me I canceled on my coven frequently too. This was becoming a pattern, a pattern I didn't like. If I couldn't find time in my life for the people I loved, what was the point?

"I'm at Tiny's Garage," I told him. "And she's dead."

A second ticked by, then another. "Repeat that." He finally said. I did.

"You're sure she's dead?"

"She's squashed under a car and there's a lot of blood and she's not breathing. Pretty sure she's dead."

"Damn." A rustling noise then the jangle of keys. "What are you doing there anyway? Shouldn't you be home, getting ready?"

"I was, then I got attacked by a Garrag and Annie turned up and saved me then she saw the Astrudian Amulet someone had left for me for my birthday and since Tiny shares a birthday with me she wanted to come here to check that Tiny hadn't been gifted an amulet as well and then... we found her. Dead." It came out in a rush, and I sucked in a gulp of air.

"I didn't get half of that." He admitted. "I'm on my way. Stay put. Don't touch anything."

Too late. But he'd already hung up. "Jackson says to stay here," I said to Gran unnecessarily. This wasn't my first death, I knew the drill.

"Do you see anything unusual? Out of the ordinary?" I asked Gran, pacing backward and forwards. Gran shook her head. "Nope. Car parts. Books on cars. Tools. Annie said she was looking for some sort of present—that the amulet may have been left for Tiny like it had been for you."

"Yeah. Maybe. I found nothing like that in the office. I wonder if Tiny has it on her?" I turned to look at Tiny. She may have stuffed a small trinket box into her coverall pockets.

"Annie searched her," Gran told me.

"She did?"

Gran nodded.

"Annie came to the house," I said.

Gran nodded. "You said."

"She told me she had concerns. About me."

Gran froze, her eyes darting to mine. She said nothing. A first for my Gran. "She seems to think I'm not all in with my magic and that if I wasn't, then she pretty much invited me to leave the coven." I couldn't believe my chin wobbled as I choked the last words out.

"She did, huh?"

"Why aren't you upset? Why aren't you outraged? Why aren't you on my side?" I cried.

"Oh sweetheart, I am. Always have been. Always will be. But you can't keep blowing the coven off. And Annie has a point, you've always been wishy-washy with your magic, not wanting to use it, almost afraid of it."

The truth hurt. They were both right, and I didn't know what to think. I didn't want to leave the coven; I liked things just the way they were, but apparently that wasn't enough for Annie. I needed to be all in or all out.

"She moves really fast for a seventy-year-old," I said, changing the subject. I needed time alone to digest everything Annie had said to me and how I felt about it.

"Seventy?" Gran snorted. "Child, that woman is over three hundred years old."

I choked. "What? How?"

Gran blew out an exasperated breath. I figured I'd just made Annie's point. I had very little idea how things worked and considering I'd been born and brought up a witch, I should know every little thing there was to know. It seemed I'd been living my witch life with my head buried in the sand.

"She's a head witch. Head witches, while not immortal, have an extended life span."

"Right." I vaguely remembered that.

"And they are gifted with extra speed and strength. Hence, she's fast. You're only just noticing this now?"

I shook my head helplessly. I had no excuse really, and I was slightly ashamed at my naivety. I needed to do better. I had to do better, or I'd be without a coven. It was a sobering thought.

Gran and I stood at the edge of the parking lot and watched as Officer Miles wrapped crime scene tape across the front of Tiny's garage.

"So it was murder." Gran looped her elbow through mine, squeezing my arm, her excitement palpable. The bald green bird sat on her shoulder.

"We already guessed that." I reminded her. We'd figured the killer had delivered a blow to her head—hence the mark on her forehead. Then her body had been staged beneath the hoist to make it look like an accident. My mind flittered to the fox who'd died beneath his tractor today. Jackson had said it wasn't suspicious, just an unfortunate accident, but knowing what I know, that he and I and Tiny all share a birthday, and while I was the only one to receive an amulet, I was the only one still alive.

"It's hardly surprising." Gran continued, and I looked at her in surprise.

"Why do you say that?"

"Duh," she replied, "Tiny was not the best-liked fairy in town. She was an absolute beeatch ninety-nine percent of the time. And her creative pricing structure has infuriated more than one customer. They only keep coming back because she's damn good at what she does. Did."

I chewed my lip, remembering the conversations I'd overheard this morning. The shifter named Weaver whose truck she held hostage, stacking on late fees and refusing to release it until he'd paid up. That must be infuriating, especially if you needed your truck to earn money to pay the bill. My eyes drifted over the workshop, landing on the spot Weaver's truck had been. Now there was nothing but the tarp, discarded on the floor. Had he returned, killed her, and taken his truck? He certainly had a motive.

Then there was the phone call, some sort of deal she'd changed her mind on. Had she agreed to sell the garage and then reneged? Was that worth killing over? It would ensure the future sale of the garage with her out of the way—but what about a will? Did Tiny have one? Who would benefit from her death? All excellent questions to which I had no answers.

Jackson spotted us, said something to Officer Miles before crossing the lot to where we stood, his brows pulled together. "This is an unfortunate business." He said.

"How did she die?" Gran asked as if it wasn't perfectly obvious.

"Too soon to tell. Now tell me again what happened today." Jackson focused his attention on me, pulling out his phone to take notes. I told him everything that had happened, from Annie turning up at my house this afternoon and saving me from the Garrag attack, to her discovery of the Astrudian Amulet, to her suggestion of checking on Tiny.

"Alice, you said you've seen a picture of the amulet that was left for Harper? Do you think you could get us a copy?"

Gran beamed at him, "Of course I can, Jackson."

"What are you thinking?" I asked.

"You said it was an artifact. Could your parents have sent it? Not realizing what it was?"

My heart dropped. "They're archeologists. Of course, they'd know what it was. They'd never send me something like that. But you can't look for it, Jackson. It's dangerous. If you or any of your officers touch it..."

He rubbed a hand up and down my arm in a soothing gesture. "We're wearing gloves. We don't know what we're dealing with yet—but I agree, it probably wasn't from your parents. But we need some facts before we go running off half-cocked."

"You're right." I sighed, leaning into him for a moment. "It's just so surreal. This morning I was here buying the oil filter and now, hours later, she's dead."

"Tell me about this morning," Jackson said. "Was anyone else here? Did Tiny seem stressed? Anything, no matter how inconsequential it may seem, can help."

I filled him in on what I knew. The shifter called Weaver. The phone call. And Roxanne Mann, the fiancée of one of the richest men in Whitefall Cove.

"Roxanne Mann?" Jackson paused, eyes narrowing. "Singh's fiancee?"

"Yup." I nodded, rocking back on my heels. It had surprised me too.

"Was her car in the garage do you know?"

I frowned. "I don't think so. The same yellow car was on the hoist, and when I left I noticed a black BMW in the parking lot that hadn't been there when I arrived—I assumed it was Roxanne's."

Jackson recorded what I'd just told him then pinned Gran with a look. "I suppose there is no point in me saying you don't need to investigate this? Believe it or not, the Whitefall Cove police department can manage without you and the murder club."

Gran clasped her chest in mock outrage, "How

many murders have we helped you solve, Detective? I'm affronted that you'd turn down our help. We are excellent investigators. Especially Harper." She added, knowing if she dragged my name into this he'd back down.

"You're a bunch of nosy women who insist on interfering with police business." He softened his words with a smile. "But seriously," his next words were directed at me. "I know you will look into this, that there's nothing I can do or say to dissuade you otherwise. So just be careful. We may have another killer on the loose. I don't want you getting hurt." He stroked his thumb over my cheek and I leaned into his hand, heart a flutter.

"I promise to be careful." I held his hand to my face, knowing how much he worried. "Could you tell us how she died?"

He barked out a laugh, playfully bopped my nose as he pulled his hand away. "Trust you to take a moment and ruin it."

I giggled. "Babe, we're standing on the edge of a crime scene, so, you know, I don't think this really classifies as a moment."

"Come on, spill." Gran prodded, ignoring our banter.

"You sure you want to know?" He asked.

We nodded in unison and leaned in closer. Jackson

looked around to make sure he wouldn't be overheard. "This goes no further, understood?" We nodded again. "Crushed by the hoist. She must have been working underneath when it either had a mechanical failure or someone intentionally released it. She had no chance of surviving three thousand pounds of car on top of her."

I shuddered. What a terrible way to die. Poor Tiny. I glanced back at the garage, caught a glimpse of yellow in between people walking backward and forwards. The car she'd been working on this morning. I'd been standing right next to it. And now Tiny was under it.

"What time did this happen, do you think?"

"ME puts time of death around four-thirty, five, give or take."

"Not particularly late then." I murmured to myself.

"What do you mean?"

"Well..." I paused while I thought out loud, "If I were planning to kill Tiny by crushing her with her own hoist, I'd at least wait until it was dark. We all know Tiny frequently works late in her garage, alone. It's still daylight at five o'clock, so you risk being seen."

"They could have rigged the hoist though." Gran pointed out. "Tampered with it so it gave away at some point."

Jackson agreed with both of us. "Both valid points. We won't know more until we've thoroughly examined the hoist. And while it wasn't dark at five, it was after closing for Tiny, she shuts up at four, and traffic in these parts is light. It would have been a risk, but doable. Especially if the perpetrator was someone who didn't look out of place, who you wouldn't have paid any attention to if you saw them."

"You're saying it was someone she knew?"

"It may not even be murder," Jackson said. "We need to wait for the report on the hoist."

"But the graze on her forehead, like someone had hit her?"

"Until we have evidence to corroborate that, we have to treat it as an accidental death."

"And you don't think two accidental deaths in one day is a coincidence?" I pointed out. "And both of them involved being crushed beneath a vehicle." It was sounding more and more like we had a serial killer in Whitefall Cove.

"How about you leave the detective work to me?" Jackson leaned down and pecked my cheek. "I need to get back to work and clear you lot out. We need to remove Tiny's body and you don't want to be around for that."

He was right; I did not. Nodding I looked around for Gran who'd wandered off, finding her standing by my car with the ugly bird on her arm. Giving Jackson a final wave I hurried to join her. It wasn't until we were back at Gran's house and the bird was happily ensconced on the back of a kitchen chair that we realized we had no supplies for it.

"I can duck out and grab some birdseed." I offered, but Gran was shaking her head. "Agnes is coming around soon for a healing session, I'll ask her to pick something up. Although..." she trailed off and had a look on her face that was either intense concentration or she needed to poop. With Gran, it could be either. "You could just drop by Tiny's house. This little guy has probably got a cage and food there. It would be nice for him to have his own things. Maybe even find out his name?"

"You're saying I should go to Tiny's house and snoop?" I narrowed my eyes. It wasn't a terrible idea. The police were busy with her garage, would they even bother with her house? And the bird was the perfect excuse.

"If the shoe fits."

And that's how I found myself sneaking down the side of Tiny's house just after dark. Her house was across the road from her garage so I'd figured it prudent to wait until the sun had gone down and I had less chance of being spotted. As it was, the garage was all locked up and deserted. I'd parked further down the street and walked up and stood for a moment gazing at the dark building, imagining what had gone on there a few hours earlier. Despite her rude and often mean demeanor, Tiny didn't deserve to die. Now at her back door, I searched around for a spare key, found one under a flower pot, and shook my head. Why did people hide keys in such findable spots? But then I guess when you're Tiny's size, you don't have to worry too much about intruders. Sliding the key into the lock I turned the handle and slipped inside.

NINE

Not wanting to draw attention to the fact that someone was snooping inside Tiny's house, I felt around in the dark, making my way to the front rooms and drawing the curtains and blinds before flicking on a light. What I saw surprised me. Her house was neat. And tidy. Unlike her garage where it was chaos, her home was unexpectedly clean. Two gigantic sofas dominated the living area, a square rustic coffee table, and massive television that took up most of one wall. The air smelled like vanilla, and I followed my nose to the kitchen. On the countertop was a rack of cupcakes. Frowning I moved closer. They looked fresh. They smelled fresh. Reaching out a hand I touched one. Still warm. What the hell?

My heart skipped a beat. Someone was here.

Someone had baked these cupcakes, and it hadn't been Tiny, and I hardly think Annie had stopped by and whipped up a batch while searching for the amulet. Standing at the kitchen counter I slowly turned my head, some sixth sense telling me I was being watched. Then I saw it, in the darkness at the end of the hallway where the light didn't reach the shadows... a pair of red eyes. What happened next wasn't my finest moment. Instead of logically processing the fact that whoever owned those red eyes hadn't harmed me, had kept their distance and was at home in Tiny's kitchen and it was I who was the trespasser... I totally panicked. With a scream I spun, my arm knocking the cooling rack and sending cupcakes sliding across the counter onto the floor. The clatter startled me even more and as I bolted, my foot came down on a cupcake, crushing it underfoot before sliding out from under the rest of my body.

I was losing my battle with gravity. Despite urging my legs to propel me toward the back door, the one that was currently sliding away at a ninety-degree angle, my brain was telling me I was about to be in a whole world of pain with torn tendons and God only knows what else unless I stopped my momentum and the only way I could think to do that was to throw myself backward. Which I did, landing with a jarring crash on my rear, my leg smarting but still attached. Heart thundering in my chest I threw a panicked look down the hallway. The red eyes blinked. "You okay?" They asked.

I nodded, not trusting my voice.

"Sorry if I startled you." The voice continued.

"Y.. y.. you're the red-eyed demon that's been stalking me." I stuttered, heart rate showing no signs of slowing as I sat unmoving on the floor.

Red eyes snorted. "Err. Stalking? I don't think so."

I swallowed, a bead of sweat trickling down my back as I calculated my chances of getting to my feet and out the back door before the demon could attack. My heart practically stopped when the hallway light flicked on and I saw for the first time the body that went with those red eyes. My worst nightmare was confirmed. He was a demon all right, no doubt about it, from the dark blueish black reptilian skin to the two horns curling out of his forehead. He was big too, about Tiny's size, which begged the question... why was he in Tiny's house baking cupcakes?

"If you must know, I was exploring." The demon continued, not making any move toward me, in fact, he looked relaxed. To lull me into a false sense of safety?

"Exploring?" I choked, trying not to hyperventilate.

"I feel you're not really listening to me." The demon complained, "You're hearing my words but you're not actively listening."

"I'm listening." I nodded, while in my head I was planning my escape, what spell to use that would send him back to his own dimension. "Wait... you came through the tear, didn't you? The breach between dimensions."

He nodded. "I did."

"But the breach was closed. They sent all the creature's back. Why are you still here?"

"I live here now."

"But..."

He took a step toward me then and I let out a little shriek, shuffled backward on my butt, and hit my head against the cupboard. In a panic, I flung out my hand, hitting him with a stream of magic.

He chuckled, "that tickles," and rubbed his chest while continuing toward me. My panic intensified as I scooted on my rear until my back hit the wall. I stretched both hands out, firing off reams of magic that appeared to delight and amuse him and do diddly squat in actually stopping him, let alone slowing him down. I was doomed. He stopped in the kitchen doorway, cocked his head, then held out his hand. "I'm Drizzach. My friends call me Driz. Can we be friends?"

My mouth dropped open, and I stared, long and hard. He waited patiently, hand outstretched while I simply stared at him. Eventually, I gathered my wits. Clearing my throat I croaked, "you want to be friends?"

He nodded, his mouth twisting into a smile. I'm sure he meant the smile to be reassuring. Instead, it looked more of a snarl, two fangs peeking into view.

"Are you friends with Tiny?" My heart was finally starting to settle into its normal rhythm, despite the gleam of his teeth I was somewhat reassured that he didn't mean to hurt me if that was his intent he would have done it by now.

"I love Tiny." He said simply. And just like that my eyes filled with tears. He loved her. And I suspect she loved him. And that's why she'd told that Mathis person on the phone she had something to stay in Whitefall Cove for. Because he was waiting for her, only she wouldn't be coming home. Not ever. A tear overflowed and trickled down my cheek. Driz noticed and crouched in front of me, close, but not touching. "You're sad." He said. "Why?"

Wiping away the tears I sniffed and looked into his red eyes, no longer glowing now that he was in the light. "Tiny's had an accident, Driz."

"She's hurt? Where is she, I must go to her!" He jumped to his feet, his head almost touching the ceiling.

"No, wait!" I scrambled to my feet, putting out a hand to stop him, snatching it back when it came into contact with his slick scales. "You can't go to her, Driz."

"No? Why?" He reminded me of a child, his ways

simple and I had to remind myself he was not of our world.

"She died." I breathed. He looked at me in silence, I waited as he processed the words, waited for his outpouring of grief—or anger—braced myself for both. He nodded once. "She's dead?" He asked.

"Yes."

"Okay."

I jerked back in surprise. Okay? I'd been expecting an outpouring of grief or a tantrum. Not his calmly spoken okay.

"You don't seem very upset—I thought you loved her?"

He nodded, "I love her very much, and I'll miss her, but I'll see her in the next world. Now that we've found each other we'll always be bound. She'll wait for me, and I'll join her when I leave this realm. It is all but a journey."

I blinked at his logic, touched at his outlook. But now I had another problem. What was I going to do with a red-eyed demon called Driz from another dimension? Then a horrible thought occurred to me.

"Are you a... crossroads demon?" I asked, chewing my lip.

"I don't know what that is." He replied as he began cleaning the mess I'd made in the kitchen, sweeping up the scattered cupcakes and depositing them in the bin. As I watched his easy smooth movements, I realized why Tiny's house was so clean and tidy. Driz. He was a domesticated demon. Humming to himself he began whipping up another batch of cupcakes while I stood helplessly watching him until my brain finally caught up with the reason I was standing in Tiny's kitchen in the first place.

"We have Tiny's bird." I blurted.

Driz didn't even glance up. "So?"

"Well... ummm... I guess you want it back?" Gran would be heartbroken, I could see she'd already bonded with the unfortunate looking creature.

Driz snorted. "No, I do not. I like it best when it is far away from me."

"Oh!"

Hearing the surprise in my voice Driz glanced up. "Tiny took it to work with her every day. I liked that. You may keep the bird, I like it better here without it."

I nodded. "Okay. Sure. Gran really seems to like it, so I guess that'll work out well for everyone. I, ummm, dropped by to see if it has a cage? Birdseed?"

"Sure. Cage is over there." Driz nodded toward the dining room where a round cage stood in one corner. "Seed and bits and pieces are in the dresser." Next to the cage was a dresser with a range of trophies displayed on the top. I wandered over to look at them. Driz noticed me looking.

"They are replicas." He said.

"Why replicas?" I noticed each one was for a different car racing event.

"Tiny was too big to be a racing car driver, so she became the best mechanic the world has ever seen," Driz said proudly. "When the first team she worked for won, they gave her a replica of the trophy as a thank you—they knew they'd never have crossed the finish line in the first place if it wasn't for Tiny. It became something of a tradition."

Opening the dresser door I peered inside. Sure enough, two bags of birdseed, a stack of old newspapers—I assumed to line the bottom of the birdcage—and a handful of toys. "What's the bird's name?" I carefully put the toys and birdseed into the cage to make for easier transportation.

"Ace." Driz replied. Then asked, "would you like a coffee?"

Now that I was getting over the shock of finding a demon in Tiny's home, one that was friendly and apparently liked to bake, I figured I could use the situation to my advantage and find out more about Tiny's home life, and search for clues as to who killed her. "Sure."

Driz's red eyes landed on the trophies again and he sighed wistfully. "She could have had a different life. She worked the racing circuit early in her career, that's where she got all her money to buy this place and the garage. Then her team, it was like they were cursed, bad luck after bad luck. Mechanical failures. And the teammates she considered family, who she'd do anything for, turned on her. Blamed her for their losses. Terminated her contract. Only word had got around and despite her indisputable skill under the hood, no one would touch her. They said she was jinxed."

"But she helped her team win all of these!" I waved a hand over the shining gold replicas of cars.

"Exactly!" Driz threw up his hands.

"These date back over twenty years ago." I noted.

Driz was nodding. "Tiny had them all shoved into a box. We had a big argument when she came home one night and saw them there."

"She didn't want them on display?"

"She didn't want reminding. The biggest hurt for Tiny wasn't losing her job, it was the pain of people you considered your family turning their back on you. She never recovered from the betrayal."

I wondered if that's when Tiny started being such a grumpy, unpleasant, difficult to deal with individual. Because those she loved and trusted most in the world had thrown her under the bus and turned their back on her. It couldn't have been easy for her being such a big fairy either, standing out, being different. Usually fairies were petite. Not Tiny. So thinking you'd found your tribe where you were accepted unconditionally and then have that torn away from you must have really done a number on her. Driz continued talking, and I tuned back in.

"I think I was sent to save her." He was saying.

"Wait, what?" I interrupted. "Back up a second. What do you mean?"

"Before I arrived, Tiny was in talks with a team, they were offering her a very lucrative contract to return to the circuit. It would have meant her selling up and being on the road year-round."

"That's a big commitment."

"They were offering big money. And she'd been about to sign when we met."

"And then things changed." I could guess where this was going. Tiny didn't want to leave her new love. Suddenly selling up and leaving Whitefall Cove to follow the racing season wasn't as appealing as it had been before the rift opened and Driz arrived.

Driz nodded, carrying two mugs of coffee over to the dining table. Easing out one of the large, chunky, wooden chairs he eased himself into it. He was huge. He looked like an adult sitting on children's furniture. I giggled a little at the visual and sat opposite him, accepting the coffee.

"Wait. This team she was about to sign with, a guy called Mathis wasn't involved was he?" I was sure that was the name Tiny had mentioned when she'd taken the call in her garage this morning, the one I'd listened in on when using the bathroom. She'd said something about a lucrative offer and changing her mind. And wishing him luck on the circuit.

"Could be. I don't know." Driz took a sip of his coffee and sighed. "I like this beverage a lot."

"Me too, Driz, me too." I agreed. Who would have thought I'd be sitting in a dead fairy's dining room drinking coffee with a demon? Not this girl, that's for sure. "Does Tiny keep any paperwork here?"

"Some." He fiddled with his coffee cup. "Why?"

"If Tiny had been about to sign, they'd have given her a contract. I wouldn't mind having a look at it, see who we're dealing with."

"Do you think they killed her? Because she changed her mind?" His shock was genuine, but I was shaking my head. "It wouldn't make sense for them to kill her. They want her on their team, not dead."

He visibly relaxed. "Makes sense. I turned the spare bedroom into a home office for Tiny. It could be in there."

"You're very... organized." I didn't want to offend, had almost said domesticated but had stopped myself before the word left my mouth. Driz didn't notice. "It gives me something to do while Tiny is at work. This place was such a mess, she is a very messy fairy. Was." He corrected, a brief flash of grief crossing his face. "We were building up to telling people I was here, and that once I was out, I would help her in the garage."

"Why did she keep you a secret all this time?"

"Because people react just the way you did. Afraid. I'm big, with dark blue scales and red eyes. They think I am here to cause harm and that is not true. And Tiny's distrust of people didn't help. She thought you would banish me back through the rift. So I stayed hidden."

"Well, the rift is closed now, so I couldn't do that even if I wanted to." But he had a point. My initial reaction had been one of fear, but to be fair, I was poking around in what I believed to be an empty house. Anyone would have scared the pants off me, demon or not. "Like it or not people will find out about you now, you can't stay hidden here."

"The people with the flashing lights will take me away?" Driz asked, a hint of worry in his voice.

"They'll want to ask you questions. They're the authorities, they're trying to find out who hurt Tiny." I really didn't know what would happen to Driz. He'd crossed here illegally from another dimension and while it was true, I couldn't send him back, the Supernatural Council probably had procedures for situations like this. Which meant calling Jackson. Which I would do as soon as I'd had a good look around myself. "But before that happens, show me Tiny's office, let's see what we can find out ourselves first."

Driz smiled. "Okay."

Driz and Tiny made an odd couple. Not only the

species thing, a fairy and a demon, but their personalities were on different ends of the scale. Tiny was mean. Driz is kind. Tiny was untidy. Driz is a neat freak. Two opposites making up a complete whole. And that saddened me more than it should have because now Tiny was dead and Driz was alone and that hardly seemed fair. I followed him down the hallway, and into the bedroom he'd converted into an office. There was a large table with an in-tray on one corner, papers neatly stacked inside. Two bookcases, one crammed full of what appeared to be mechanical books, journals and magazines. The other bookcase housed an impressive collection of thriller paperbacks.

Crossing to the desk I pulled out the chair and sat. From this vantage point, I could see directly across the road to the garage.

"Could you pull the blinds?" I asked Driz. "Best not advertise that we're in here."

"But you said the authorities needed to know about me." He pointed out.

"You're right, I did. But first I want to see if we can find that contract because if the authorities get their hands on it first, they'll probably seize it as evidence and then we won't know what was in it."

"I don't know what any of that means," Driz admitted, pulling the blind down and blocking us from view from anyone passing by. "I am going back to the kitchen to check on the cupcakes."

I nodded absently, not really listening as I pulled the in-tray in front of me and began leafing through the papers. Utility bills, flyers for the local market, a bank statement. Then, about halfway through the pile, I found it. The contract. It was ten pages long and full of legalese. I snapped a picture of each page. Gran and I could go over it later, I may even show it to Jenna who's a reporter and probably has more of an idea than I do on what it all means. But I got one thing of interest from it. The contract was between Tiny and Jessie Mathis. Now I had a thread to pull, a connection to follow. Tiny may have turned down the offer but negotiations weren't dead and buried. Not judging by the phone call yesterday and the fact that the contract was still sitting on Tiny's desk, unsigned.

Sliding the paper clip back onto the contract I put it to one side and continued going through the rest of the in-tray, then the drawers of the desk and finally the bookcase, finding nothing more of interest I headed back to the kitchen where the smell of freshly baked cupcakes wafted in the air.

"Did you find what you were looking for?" Driz asked from the sink where he was busy washing up.

"I did, thank you."

"Please, have a cupcake—they're not iced yet, and be careful, they're hot."

"Driz? I'm going to have to call the authorities now. Let them know you're here."

He paused, his hands submerged in soap suds. "Okay." It hit me then, the trust he'd put in me, a stranger who'd come into his home uninvited and who was now turning him over to the police. He trusted me, trusted that I was doing the right thing. I only hoped I was, for strangely enough, this navy colored demon with red eyes was growing on me.

"You are where?"

The phone call to Jackson was going just as I expected. Badly. I sighed, "I'm at Tiny's house and before you get the wrong idea, I only came to pick up the cage and birdseed for that sorry excuse for a parrot that Gran has taken under her wing."

"Right." There was a pause and a rustle. I imagined he was running his hand through his hair. Probably pulling the strands out. "And there's a demon there? Called Driz? Who was Tiny's... lover?" He repeated everything I'd just told him as if saying it out loud made it more plausible.

"Yes." Driz was busy in the kitchen, icing the cupcakes, happily humming to himself.

"And you're safe?" Jackson's voice dropped, belying his concern.

"Perfectly," I assured him. "But could you come on your own? Driz has done nothing wrong and having a patrol car turn up with lights and sirens would distress him." It was partly true. I wanted Jackson to meet Driz first before he reported him to the Council. Maybe we could petition them for Driz to seek asylum with us since he couldn't return to his own realm now that the rift had been closed. Despite my initial fear when I'd seen his red eyes glowing in the dimness of the hallway, now that I'd spent some time with him I was convinced there was nothing to fear.

"I'll see you in a few minutes." I couldn't tell if Jackson was angry or worried or both. Probably both, although he should know me by now—I couldn't walk away from a good mystery and Tiny's murder was turning out to be just that. Lowering the phone to the table I watched Driz as he moved around the kitchen. Then he stopped and looked at me. "If I had known, if I had gotten to her before she died, perhaps I could have saved her?"

"Oh Driz, no, I'm sorry. No one could have saved her." I told him. She'd been doomed as soon as that car had fallen on her. Even if Driz had lifted it off of her, her injuries had been too severe.

"Driz, has anyone else been here today?" My mind went back to what Annie had said before leaving the garage, that she was coming to Tiny's house to search for the amulet. And Rupert was a demon sniffer dog, there was no way Driz would have been able to remain inside the house and undetected.

Driz shook his head. "No-one came today."

Which then begged the question, where did Annie go? She'd said she was coming here but didn't turn up. Did she go home? And if she did, why? She'd been in a burning hurry to search for another amulet. What had changed?

We both heard the car pull into the driveway and Driz's red eyes shot to mine. "It's okay. It's Jackson. He's here to help you and to find out who killed Tiny. You can trust him." Bold words, I hoped Jackson wouldn't let me down. It would be easy enough to simply pass Driz's case on to the Council and have him taken into custody as an illegal.

The back door opened and Jackson stepped inside, his eyes sweeping over me before coming to rest on Driz who remained in the kitchen, a plate of yellow iced cupcakes in his hands. He held the plate toward Jackson. "Cupcake?"

A tense few seconds ticked by, my eyes darting between Jackson and Driz as they assessed each other. Jackson sniffed the air, his eyes drifted to the cupcakes being proffered, and he took a step forward. "Those smell good."

"Driz is a bit of a domestic goddess," I said from my seat at the table, accepting one of the cupcakes and taking a bite, closing my eyes as the heavenly explosion of vanilla and strawberry exploded on my tongue. Mouth full I turned to Driz, "These are really good! Did you make them from scratch or out of a box?"

"I don't know what out of a box means." Driz placed the plate of cupcakes on the table and returned to the kitchen, wiping down the already spotless counter.

"You could have warned me he was naked." Jackson took the seat opposite me. I glanced toward the dark scaled demon who stood behind the kitchen counter.

"He has no..." I trailed off.

Driz, who had been listening, completed my sentence. "My genitalia is on the inside. Unlike your species who have it on the outside. In the males at least." He added.

"See?" I whispered to Jackson, "I haven't been ogling him." I felt my cheeks flush at the thought.

"I was going to say," he said, voice droll, "that if I'd known I'd have brought some clothes for him. Because if he wants to assimilate into our world, he will have to be clothed. At least in public."

"Oh. Right."

"Coffee?" Driz asked. "Tiny liked coffee very much. She drank a lot of it. Would you like some?"

Jackson's mouth twisted into a half-smile. "Sure, why not," and shoved the rest of his cupcake into his mouth. "So," he said when he'd finished chewing. "What did you find?"

"Find?" I blinked, feigning innocence.

He snorted. "Sure Harper, like you haven't had a good snoop around. Come on, fess up. You've probably already got a suspect list forming in that pretty little head of yours."

Okay, so I had snooped around and yes, I did have a growing suspect list. My eyes darted to Driz and Jackson followed my gaze, one eyebrow arched.

"No," I hissed. "I don't think he's involved. I mean, should we be talking about this in front of him? She was his partner, they were in love." Again I felt all misty-eyed and a lump of emotion lodged in my throat. It was so sad and I blinked rapidly to dispel the excess moisture in my eyes.

Jackson reached across the table and clasped my hand in his, rubbing his thumb in a soothing gesture across the back of my hand.

"I'm reasonably confident Driz isn't a suspect." He told me.

"Oh?" I blinked again, hopeful that this meant Jackson wasn't going to arrest Driz. Not that I'd really thought he would. Well, I was reasonably confident, but it did look suspect that Driz hadn't contacted anyone when Tiny didn't come home, and he'd have had to have seen all the excitement at the garage and hadn't come forward. But on the other hand, I could see it from Driz's point of view. He was in a strange land full of strange people. He didn't know our ways and Tiny had more than likely drummed it into him to stay hidden, that it would be bad for him if anyone saw him.

"Look at the size of him. As tall as Tiny at least, almost as broad. Whoever took Tiny down was smaller..." he trailed off, mindful of the demon in the kitchen who was quietly singing You Are My Sunshine under his breath.

"So my theory was correct." I took another cupcake, God, they were delicious. "Has the ME done the autopsy yet?" I asked.

"Preliminary examination confirms it. Despite the crush injuries sustained to her legs and abdomen, there was bruising and abrasions to the skin behind her knees, consistent with being hit with something hard. And the head injury confirms it. Tiny had a fractured skull. They hit her from behind. Whoever did it didn't think it through."

"I don't know, it looked convincing to me." I protested, wincing as I remembered the sight of Tiny pinned beneath the car as it flashed into my mind.

"A blow to the back of the legs would have made her stagger forward, most likely fall to her knees," Jackson explained. "But Tiny would recover quickly from that. They needed her temporarily—or permanently—disabled. Tiny sustained a fractured skull. A blow to the back of the head. But not from falling on the concrete. ME suggested a cylindrical-shaped object was used."

"But she was on her back when we found her. If someone hit her on the back of the head, she would have fallen forward." I could see where this was going and Jackson confirmed it.

"Staged. She was probably killed exactly where we found her, working under the car. Someone crept up on her, delivered the blow to her legs, then the one to the back of her head. Then it was just a case of rolling her into position, releasing the hoist and let the car do the rest."

"Do you think she felt it? The car?" I whispered, horrified.

Jackson shook his head. "The blow to the back of her head was fatal. Dead before she hit the ground."

Driz returned to the table carrying Jackson's coffee.

"Thanks," Jackson nodded to the cupcakes. "This is all great."

"Thank you. I like to serve." Driz smiled, played hostess, and offered Jackson the crystal bowl full of sugar cubes. "Are you going to lock me away? Tiny told me if anyone discovered I was here I'd be sent away. Locked up."

"I don't think that's necessary." Jackson took a sip of his coffee. "I'll call the Council and find out what the process is, but in the meantime, it's best you stay here, don't go venturing outside alone. The townsfolk are spooked after what happened recently with the rift, they may not give you a warm welcome."

Driz nodded. "I'm used to staying hidden."

"Tell me about you and Tiny." Jackson offered. "How did this all come about?"

I sat back and sipped my coffee while Driz recounted the story he'd already told me, how he'd seen the rift and had been curious and stepped through. One of the first people he'd seen had been Tiny, and it had been love at first sight. Then the rift had closed, and Driz had remained behind.

The two of them talked for quite some time before Jackson finally nodded his head in satisfaction, snapped a photo of Driz, then turned his attention to me. "So?" He asked. "What did you find?"

"A contract, a very lucrative one, offering Tiny a position of chief mechanic for the Mathis motor racing team."

"And that's relevant how?"

"Because when I was in Tiny's garage this morning, using the bathroom, I overheard her on the phone to Mathis and she was telling him circumstances had changed and she wasn't signing the contract. And now that I know about Driz, I think he's the reason she's not signing. Before he turned up, she'd been prepared to close up shop and hit the road, following the racing circuit for God only knows how many months a year. But that all changed with Driz's arrival. She didn't want to leave anymore, she had something to stay for."

Jackson frowned. "So you think Mathis is involved in her murder?"

But I was already shaking my head, "Actually, no, I don't. Because he wanted her to sign, so why kill her? If anything, he'd have been better off killing Driz!"

Driz stiffened in his seat.

"No offense." I blurted, belatedly realizing how blunt I'd been. "I'm just saying, Mathis does not have a motive for murder."

"But this man, Mathis." Driz said, "He doesn't know about me. Maybe he was angry with Tiny?"

"I'm sure he was angry with her, yes." I agreed.

Jackson cut in. "But enough to kill her? Harper's right. It was in his best interests to keep her alive. Who else have you got?" The twinkle in his eye told me he already had his own list of suspects and he was merely humoring me.

"That just leaves Roxanne Mann," I replied. "The fiancée of the richest man in Whitefall Cove."

ELEVEN

I failed to come up with any motive for why Roxanne would want Tiny dead. Instead, I'd packed up my car with the parrot cage and birdseed, told Driz I'd call on him tomorrow, and kissed Jackson a very long and thorough kiss goodnight. He promised to reschedule our romantic date and that I'd get a birthday do-over. He also warned me again, to leave the investigating to the police. We both knew I wouldn't, but it was cute that he'd said it, anyway.

"Gran, I'm back." Opening the front door to Gran's house I stepped into utter mayhem. Ace, the ugliest bird in the world, was clinging to the hallway light fitting, screeching at the top of his lungs, "don't touch that!" while Gran was beneath him, trying to coax him down. Archie sat a few feet away, licking his lips, his eyes trained on Ace, not so much as a blink.

"Archie? You aren't frightening Ace are you?" I scolded, setting the cage down and closing the front door behind me just in case the bird bolted.

Mreow? Archie tilted his head as if to say who me? And looked affronted that I'd even suggest such a thing. Gran was trying to coerce Ace into releasing the light fitting and perch on her arm, her voice ten octaves higher than usual, so high it hurt my ears—I hated to think what it was doing to Ace and Archie.

"Gran!" I shouted, finally getting her attention.

"About time you got back." She grumbled, planting both hands on her hips she sent me a scorching look as if this complete debacle was my fault. "Can't get the bird down." As if I needed an explanation. Every picture on the wall was askew and the vase that had been sitting on the hallway table was now in pieces on the floor.

"Yelling won't help." I said, doing my best to stay calm. I didn't like birds at the best of times, it was something about their eyes. And beaks. And talons. I shuddered. "His name is Ace," I added. Picking up the cage I shoved it at her. "Why don't you try this? He'll probably feel safer in there than he does flapping around your hallway with a cat sitting beneath him."

"Fair point." Gran conceded, taking the cage from me.

I watched Gran try to coax Ace into the cage. "Take the other stuff out of the cage first. He only needs a small amount of seed, not the entire packet. I just put it in there to make it easier to carry."

Gran glanced at the cage, and frowned, then gave a little sniff. "I knew that." Setting the cage down she huffed as she removed the seed and spare newspapers out. Ace resumed his screeching, and an answering pounding took up behind my eyes. I snatched up the cage, thrust it into Gran's arms, and said curtly, "hold the door open." She blinked at me but did as instructed. Thrusting my hand toward Ace I sent out my magic, wrapped it around the bird and gently guided him into the cage. Gran snapped the door shut behind him.

"You did it!" She beamed.

"Now will you please go put him in your bedroom?" I pleaded, "I can't hear myself think over his darn squawking."

Gran looked at Ace. "She never did like birds." Then headed upstairs, carrying the cage with her, Archie hot on her heels. I made myself comfortable in the living room.

"Right!" Gran bustled back in, dusting her hands together. "Now that's taken care of, drinks?" She pivoted and headed toward the kitchen where the alcohol was stashed. "Harper!" She yelled, "why don't you call up the murder club?"

Knowing there was no way Gran would let this go, I summoned the clue board from its hiding place in my bookstore. A second later it appeared in Gran's living room. I sent a message to Monica and Jenna, my best friends, and murder club members. Within seconds they'd both replied saying they'd be right over—I suspected they'd been waiting by their phones waiting for my message.

"Oh goody, it's here." Gran returned carrying a tray with four whiskey glasses, setting it down with a thunk on the coffee table before handing a glass to me and taking one herself. She seated herself in the chair I'd just vacated and looked at me expectantly. "Well?" She said. "Get on with it."

"Let's wait for the others to arrive first shall we?" I took a sip, the whiskey burning a fiery trail down my throat. I'd been expecting to drink bubbles tonight and celebrate my birthday, instead here I was bolting down whiskey and calling a meeting of the murder club. I listened as Gran chatted about nothing in particular but mostly about her part-time role at Drixworths. She only had two classes a week, not exactly taxing, and I wondered if that was part of the problem, why she had so much trouble sticking to the curriculum... because she had too much time on her hands.

As soon as Jenna and Monica arrived, I called the meeting to order.

"Tiny, our giant fairy, was murdered—yet it was set up to look like an accident." I began. "So it was pre-mediated. Whoever did this put some thought into it ahead of time."

"Not necessarily," Jenna argued. "Tiny was not well-liked, in fact, it's almost as if she took great delight in pissing people off."

"That's true." Monica agreed.

Jenna continued, "so whoever did this may have visited her garage for a legitimate reason, something Tiny did or said was enough to make them snap. She was under the car, doesn't take too much imagination to think if that car were to fall, she'd be crushed."

"But why hit her first? Why not just release the hoist?" Monica asked.

"Because they weren't convinced that would actually kill her," Jenna said. "Can you imagine how furious Tiny would be if that were to happen, and she didn't die? She'd heal, and then she'd come after you and she was more than capable of ripping your limbs off."

I nodded. "Fair point. If in the spur of the moment, you decided to kill Tiny, you had to make it stick. You figure belting her over the head is a good way to do it. But she's tall. You can't reach—"

"So you take her out at the knees. Topple her." Monica cut in.

"Exactly. As soon as she hits the ground, whammo,

knock her out, then hit the button on the hoist to release it, crushing her." Gran finished.

"So the question is, who was in the garage today?" I asked.

"You were." Gran pointed out.

I snorted. "Thanks Gran, hopefully this time I'm not a suspect hmmm?"

"Any reason you'd want Tiny dead?" Gran shot back. I shook my head. "Nope. I had no beef with her. Here's what I know." I picked up four post-it notes and stuck them to the board. "She spoke with Jessie Mathis. She had an unsigned contract to join his racing team, and he was pressuring her into signing." I wrote Jessie's name on a post-it. "But so far I can't find a motive for why he'd want to kill her. He needed her alive, but we can't rule out a rival team wanting to stop her from joining his team."

"Fair point." Jenna agreed, leaning back in her chair and sipping her whiskey as she watched me work.

"Then we have Glen Weaver." I added his name to a post-it. "He owes Tiny for repairs to his truck. She was holding his truck hostage until he paid up— adding late fees and interest to his account so he was getting further and further into debt with her. From what I overheard, he sells his own produce at the markets and needs his truck to transport them, so without his truck, he has no income."

"Catch twenty-two. And a definite motive." Monica said.

"Agreed. Did he return later in the day to kill her? His truck was there this morning when he made a payment, I heard her tell him he still had over a thousand dollars owing and he'd given her a hundred in cash this morning—although she fleeced him and said it was only eighty."

"That must've made him angry." Gran tsked.

"It did. And it wasn't fair. She was mean to him." I agreed. "Then we have the owner of the car she was working on, Jodie Bell. But I don't know if she was in the garage today, I didn't see her this morning and Tiny was already working on her car, she may have dropped it off the day before."

"Would you really crush your mechanic with your own car?" Gran asked. "That'd be some bad karma right there. I wouldn't want to drive it again that's for sure."

I shivered at the thought. "Who knows? But for now, she goes on the board. And then we have Roxanne Mann. I passed her walking in as I was leaving Tiny's." I wrote Roxanne's name on the board with the three others.

Gran whistled. "Why would she be going to Tiny's Garage?" She asked. "I'm sure her and Carson have people to manage that sort of thing."

"What do you mean?" Monica frowned. Gran

snorted and took a swig of whiskey. "Only that miss hoity-toity Roxanne Mann is engaged to Whitefall Cove's richest bachelor, Carson Singh. There's no way they'd take their precious BMW's to Tiny's Garage—they probably have their cars serviced in the city or something ridiculous, and they certainly wouldn't bother themselves with such mundane activities. They have staff for that."

Monica's eyebrows shot up. "They're that rich?"

I nodded. "Yep. Loaded. I was surprised to see her there, that's for sure."

Jenna was eyeballing the murder board. "Are those the only suspects?"

"It's all I have. But other people could have been in the garage today that I don't know about, which is why I want to talk to Jackson and see what I can find out. But, there's something else. After we discovered Tiny's body we had a look around, and in her office was a cash tin—inside the tin? Thousands of dollars. I can't say for sure how much, but there were handfuls of hundred dollar bills in that tin, much more than what she had invoices for. Now Tiny may be big and mean but she's not stupid. She's built up a very successful business and she wouldn't leave cash like that lying around."

"You think the cash turned up today?" Jenna guessed, and I nodded.

"She takes her cash tin home with her each night to balance the books."

"Are you sure?" Monica frowned. "How do you know she takes it home with her?"

"Oh, that's right. I haven't told you the best part." I looked around at their expectant faces. "There's a demon living in Tiny's house. They're in love."

TWELVE

After a full second of silence, they all spoke at once and I shushed them with a wave of my hand.

"His name is Driz. He came through when we had the breach between dimensions." I shot a glance at Gran before continuing. "He met Tiny and something between them just clicked. She's been hiding him at her house ever since—they were planning to petition the Council for him to stay permanently."

Gran snorted. "Bit of a coincidence don't you think? There's a new demon in town, in hiding, and then on your birthday, Harper, you receive an Astrudian Amulet."

"A what now?" Monica cut in, her eyes darting from me to Gran and back again. "What's been going on? What aren't you telling us?"

"Okay, okay, everything is fine. I was left a gift on my doorstep this morning, it turns out it's an Astrudian Amulet or demon coin. Annie saved me from touching it."

"What would have happened if she'd touched it?" Jenna asked, phone out and already googling.

"Her soul would have been marked for the crossroads demon," Gran said. Both Monica and Jenna blinked in surprise, looked at each other, then back at me. "So this is... attempted murder?" Jenna breathed.

I nodded. "I guess."

"Wait," Monica eyeballed Gran. "You're saying this is linked? This coin thing and Tiny's death? That what? You're the intended victim? Then how the hell did Tiny end up dead?"

"I'm not saying that all." Gran held up one hand and ticked off on her fingers. "We have a murdered fairy, we have an Astrudian Amulet meant for Harper, and we have a secret demon that's been hiding in our town, under our very noses, for weeks. What if this demon is hungry? What if he needs souls to survive? What do we know about him, anyway?"

"All fair questions." I tried to ease the tension in the room. "Jackson is aware of the situation and has made contact with the Council. They'll investigate of course, but Driz didn't strike me as malicious, hell he was baking cupcakes and cleaning Tiny's house."

Monica snorted. "Doesn't sound like much of a threat."

"What does a crossroads demon look like?" Jenna asked.

"They take the form of a human when they're on earth. They intentionally appeal to whoever is summoning them. Male, female, young, old." Gran replied.

"Well, Driz certainly isn't a crossroads demon." I practically sagged in relief. "He's big, almost as tall as Tiny. He has blue-black scales, red eyes, and two little horns on his head. He looks as scary as heck but he's really a sweetie." I couldn't believe how quickly the demon had won me over.

"I've got to meet him!" Gran declared, clapping her hands together. I couldn't contain my smile. "I was thinking the same thing, Gran. I'll take you over to Tiny's house tomorrow."

"Oh... do you think he'll want Ace back?" Gran asked, suddenly crestfallen. I shook my head. "No. He most certainly does not. He made it pretty clear he's not a fan of Ace, you can keep him."

"Goody." Gran clapped again and bounced in her seat. I held up a hand to calm her, "But... the coins could be related. While we didn't find one in Tiny's Garage, one was found on Del, the fox shifter who died today." I shot a glance at Jenna. "And who, coincidentally, shares a birthday with me and Tiny."

Monica shot up from the couch and moved with vampiric speed to the murder board, rapidly pinning post-it notes. I took her seat and looked at the board. She'd added the information about the coins and the link between Del, Tiny, and myself.

"But you're saying Tiny didn't have a coin?" Jenna asked.

"We didn't find one," I confirmed. "I'm wondering if she had it on her person. I know Annie searched her, but maybe it was in the pocket of her coveralls? Pinned beneath the car."

Gran narrowed her eyes. "It's a possibility." She tapped her lip, deep in thought. "Rupert may have missed sniffing it out because of all the blood."

"So, what's next?" Monica piped up.

I looked at the board, my mind a whirl as I considered our next steps. "Okay, I've got it." I eventually said. "Jenna, can you follow up on the Roxanne Mann angle? See if you can find out what she was doing at the Garage this morning?"

"Sure." Jenna agreed. "I can say I'm doing a piece for the paper—pretty sure she'll go for it, her and Carson don't shy away from publicity."

"What shall I do?" Monica asked.

"How about you come with me out to the fox's compound? I want to see if Weaver's truck is there."

"Absolutely. Tonight?"

I nodded. "We'll finish up here and then head out."

Glen Weaver was my leading suspect and having Monica as backup and witness in case things went pear-shaped was a comfort.

"What shall I do?" Gran asked.

"I want to take you out to meet Driz in the morning, before I go to work," I told her. "He'll need clothes and advice about assimilating into the community. You don't have any classes tomorrow, so you can spend the day with him if you want. But," I warned, "Jackson has asked that he doesn't leave the property. Not until everything has been squared away with the Council."

I took a sip of my whiskey and looked around the room—everyone had a job to do and seemed to be bursting at the seams to get on with it. I almost giggled. "Okay, murder club adjourned." I told them, "I'll be at the bookstore tomorrow, we'll meet again after closing."

I had the worst ever case of deja vu as my car rolled to a halt on the highway alongside the fox's compound. I'd killed the lights a mile back, and it reminded me of the night I'd snuck out here with Jenna when we were investigating another fox, Lexi Sawyer. Sliding out from behind the wheel I closed the door as silently as possible and looked at Monica over the roof of my car.

"Now what?" She asked.

"We find Weaver. I know he lives here somewhere, that he grows produce here too, so maybe look for a trailer with veggie plots or glasshouses or something."

"What are we looking for? Exactly?"

"Anything of interest. I want to be sure it was his truck that was taken from Tiny's Garage." Why anyone else would take it is beyond me, but if Weaver killed Tiny and took his truck, it was a pretty dumb move.

I could just make out Monica nodding through the darkness. She moved swiftly and silently, suddenly appearing by my side and taking my hand, making me gasp. "Here. I'll guide you, no need for a flashlight when you have impeccable night vision."

We moved stealthily through the compound, darting from junk pile to junk pile, Monica peeping through windows of trailers and cabins. I'd been about to give up, thinking I was mistaken and maybe Weaver didn't live out here at all and simply used the compound as a postal address when Monica returned to my side, excitement radiating off her in waves. "There's a big ass glasshouse back here, with a crapola camper and a beaten up old truck. I think this might be it."

I sagged in relief and clasped her hand once more as she led me through the darkness and towards what I hoped was Weaver's abode. The moon peeked out from behind the clouds, offering a brief show of illumination as we stood at the front of the truck.

"Well?" Monica whispered. "Is this it?"

"I'm an idiot." I whispered back. "The truck I saw in Tiny's Garage was under a tarp. I have no idea if it was this truck or not."

"But chances are it is." Monica hissed. "Think about it. Weaver told her he needed the truck to move his produce—meaning he had no other vehicle. Hence, this must be his truck. It must be the one that was in Tiny's Garage."

"You're right. Let me snap a photo of the plates, see if I can match it up with any of Tiny's paperwork. You go check, see if he's in his trailer."

She sped off silently; the moon dipped behind the clouds once more and I was in total darkness. I snapped a photo of the license plate then crept along the side of the truck, peeking in the side window. I wasn't looking for anything specific, just curious, so color me surprised when a glance in the back of the bed had me freezing in place. Blinking I tried to focus on the object lying in the back, cursing my limited vision.

"Monica?" I whispered, knowing she'd hear me with her super vampire senses. She was by my side a second later. "You called?" She asked.

I pointed to the back of the truck. "What's that?"

She leaned over the tailgate to take a look. "A big

ass metal pole." She said. Then she sniffed, long and deep, sucking air up into her nostrils. "And it has blood on it." Her head swiveled in my direction. "You don't think?"

"Hey! What's going on out here? Who are you and what are you doing with my truck?" A flashlight beam hit me fair in the face. I lifted my arm to block the glare.

"It's Harper Jones," I called out. "Sorry to disturb you."

The flashlight lowered from my face and I blinked, trying to clear the spots of light still dancing in my vision.

"Shoulda figured you'd be out here poking around sooner or later," Weaver grumbled, spinning on his heel he headed back to his trailer. "Better come in."

I glanced at Monica, who shrugged, then followed Weaver into his trailer. The last trailer I had been in belonged to Llewellyn Cox, demon hunter, and this was nothing compared to Llewellyn's. While Llewellyn had a lot of herbs and potions, they were neat and organized. Weaver's trailer was a red hot mess, and the stench made my nose twitch. Had he ever cleaned this place? Dishes were stacked in the sink, a quick glance confirmed several were covered in mold. I shuddered, making a mental note not to touch anything.

"I know why you're here." Weaver huffed, sliding

his wiry frame in between the bench seat and table. "Sit!" He ordered, indicating the seat opposite. The seat was piled high with clothing, having spilled off the mountain of laundry on the table. I could practically see body odor fumes radiating from it.

"That's okay, I'll stand."

"Suit yourself. Spit out whatever it is you've come to say, then leave me in peace."

I shot a glance at Monica, who was standing in the open doorway, head slightly turned to breathe in the fresh night air—I could only imagine how the foul smell of his trailer was affecting her sensitive nose.

"Very well." I cleared my throat. "I wanted to ask you about your truck. It was at Tiny's Garage this morning—I was there when you made a repayment, I heard your argument with Tiny. So I'm really curious as to how your truck is here, parked outside, now? That is your truck, isn't it?" I nodded my head in the general direction of the vehicle in question.

"Who says I didn't pay out my debt with that fairy?" He crossed his arms across his chest.

"Did you?" My eyebrows shot into my hairline. Maybe someone had lent him the money, Tiny had been cashed up when she'd died.

Weaver deflated like a burst balloon. "No." He sighed.

"Ahhhh." I pursed my lips. "But you did go back to the garage again today, yes?"

Weaver's bleary eyes met mine, defeat written all over him, in the slump of his shoulders, the downturn of his lips. His hands fell to the table, palms up. "I did." He admitted.

"Did you kill Tiny?" I asked.

He shook his head. "No, she was dead when I got there." I blinked in shock. My eyes darted to Monica and then back to Weaver. "Wait. So you went back to the garage, to what? Argue with Tiny some more, try to convince her to let you have your truck back? But she was dead—and you didn't tell anyone? Call the authorities?"

"I was in shock, all right." He said defensively, "I was all worked up ready to have it out with her and I walk in and there she is, underneath a car, squished like a bug. Dead as a doornail she was. Radio still playing. I panicked, figured I'd take my truck and get out of there. Darned parrot nearly gave me a heart attack when I went into the office to get my keys."

I looked down at the floor, gathering my thoughts, idly examining the torn, stained linoleum. "Were the garage doors up or down when you arrived?" I asked, toeing at the edge of the linoleum.

"Both doors were up." He replied. "I closed them behind me after I got my truck out. Couldn't get the second one all the way down and I was starting to really freak out by then so I just hightailed it out of there."

"You didn't think to call the police?" I lifted my head and pinned him to his seat with a glare.

"They'd think I did it." He protested. I shook my head, poor Tiny.

"Did you know there's a metal pole covered in blood in the tray of your truck?" Monica said conversationally.

Weaver jumped to his feet. "What? No. That can't be. I did not kill Tiny, I swear."

I acted on pure reflex, my magic shooting out and pinning Weaver to the wall. "No sudden moves," I warned him. To Monica, I said, "call Jackson."

THIRTEEN

The arrest of Glen Weaver for the murder of Tiny the giant fairy was all over town the following morning. Gran was buzzing with anticipation when I picked her up to take her to Tiny's.

"Tell me everything!" She demanded, sliding into the passenger seat, scooping Archie onto her lap as she did so. They'd learned to compromise on who rode shotgun. When Gran was with us, Archie merely sat on her lap. I'm pretty sure he preferred it, for it gave him a height advantage to see out the window. When Gran wasn't with us, Archie got the seat to himself.

"I already did. Last night." I reminded her. After the police had arrived at the compound, seized Weaver's truck, the murder weapon, and arrested him, I'd had to endure a lecture from Jackson about not poking my nose into police investigations and something about having no boundaries when it came to my own personal safety. He'd then grinned, told me "well done", and dropped a rather passionate kiss on my lips. When he finally pulled away I'd looked up to see the cold as ice stare of Officer Liliana Miles aimed my way. I don't know what possessed me, but I winked at her. *Winked!* Way to poke the bear, Harper. Liliana is Jackson's ex, and despite the fact that Jackson and I have been an item for months now, she still dislikes me with a passion. Though to be fair, I think she disliked me long before Jackson and I became a couple, but when he broke up with her and began dating me? That just cemented things for her.

I stifled a yawn as I pulled into the driveway of Tiny's house. It had been a late night and since today was Wendy's day off and my turn to open the store, there were no sleep-ins. I clasped Gran's wrist before she could get out of the car. "Remember. No leaving the house. No leading Driz astray—he's new to our world, he doesn't understand the rules." Gran slapped a palm to her chest in mock outrage. "Who me? Lead him astray?" She shook off my hold and climbed out of the car, "I wouldn't be doing my job right if I didn't." She slammed the door before I could respond.

Shaking my head, I followed, carrying the box of fabric she'd brought with her. Whether Driz liked it or not he was about to be bedazzled by Gran. She'd dressed down for today's meeting with the demon, if you could call gold metallic leggings, rainbow-striped fluffy ugg boots, a white skin-tight tank that was several sizes too small and revealed her navel and the piercing that glinted in the light, and a black leather jacket that I'd never seen in rotation before, dressing down. Her hair was dyed blue and black and she had more gold chains around her neck than Mr. T.

Archie trotted beside us as we made our way to the rear of the house. Driz must have heard us arrive for the door opened as we climbed the steps of the back porch and he beamed at me.

"Harper!" He greeted. "You came back!"

I smiled. "I said I would. Driz, this is my Gran." I introduced them, "Gran, this is Driz."

"Pleased to meet you, Gran." Driz reached out and plucked the box out of my grasp. "Let me take that. Come in. I have coffee."

I practically drooled. Today was going to be a multiple caffeine day and I'd gratefully take what I could get. "What's that smell? Have you been baking again?" I followed my nose, the scent dancing on the air divine. Sitting on the kitchen bench was what looked to be a cherry pie. I leaned over, getting a face full of steam, and took another sniff. There was cherry, but something else I couldn't quite pinpoint.

Driz placed the box at the end of the dining table and joined me in the kitchen. "I have." He nodded. "Cherry Pie. Tiny has a tree out back." He pointed out the back window.

"What else is in it?" I asked, "it smells delicious."

Driz looked puzzled. "Nothing unusual. I followed the recipe in the book." He pointed to a dog eared recipe book by the sink. I blinked in surprise. I hadn't even known Tiny liked to cook, let alone had a massive cherry tree in her garden ripe for harvesting. But then given Tiny's temperament, it wasn't surprising I knew very little about her, she wasn't one to encourage familiarity.

"You certainly are a big boy." Gran looked Driz up and down, "you know what would look good on you and those scales?" She continued, rummaging through the box to pull out a bolt of red sequined fabric. "Red."

The fabric caught Driz's attention and he was across the room in a flash, holding the fabric up to his chest, oohing and ahhing with Gran before the pair of them dove back into the box. I rolled my eyes. I could see where this was heading. Gran was going to create a demon mini-me, and Driz, bless his heart, was going to let her.

"Guys, I've got to get going. Gran, call if you need anything."

Driz spun to face me, the biggest smile on his face.

"Thank you for being my friend, Harper Jones." He wrapped me in a hug, his big arms gentle, his scales surprisingly warm. "Please, take the pie with you. I baked it for you."

"Hey!" Gran protested, "what about me? I like pie."

"I will bake you a pie too," Driz told her and I swear Gran practically swooned. Archie, sensing there would be tasty morsels in his future, opted to stay with Gran when I called him from the back door, walking away from me with his tail in the air. Couldn't say I blamed him, my stomach was telling me to stay too.

"You two have fun. I'll swing by after work to pick you up, Gran." I accepted the pie Driz handed me, along with a travel mug full of coffee. I assumed this was his routine with Tiny, sending her off with coffee and food every morning.

"Yeah, yeah." She waved me away, pulling out a ream of purple tulle to wrap around Driz's waist before frowning and casting it aside. "Need more contrast."

Shaking my head, I let myself out. I had a feeling Driz and Gran were going to be the best of friends—providing we could get the Council to agree to him staying. I wasn't sure what would happen to him if they said no. The rift had closed to his realm, so I assumed the Council would contact a druid, maybe even Finn Hurley, to create a doorway back to Driz's dimension.

"You wouldn't know anything about missing evidence would you?" Jackson asked conversationally. I held the phone away from my ear and frowned at it, of course Jackson couldn't see my response so putting the phone back to my ear, I demanded, "what are you even talking about? What missing evidence? I've been in the bookstore all day. All day. It's Wendy's day off, I haven't set foot outside since opening this morning." I'd only just flipped the open sign over to closed. Business had been brisk, which made the day go fast, but most of the customers had been locals wanting to know the gossip on Tiny's murder. Thankfully I had Driz's cherry pie for sustenance. That, and coffee.

"The Astrudian Amulet we found on Del. It's missing."

"Oh." This wasn't good. I'd bet money Annie was behind the missing amulet. Should I tell Jackson I thought Annie may be responsible? Or protect Annie— after all, the amulets were dangerous, if anyone touched them with bare hands they'd quickly find themselves minus one soul.

"Missing?" I repeated, mind frantic. "Did you end up finding one on Tiny?"

"Actually, we did." He replied. Damn. Three amulets, all delivered to three people who shared the same birthday. But by whom? And why?

"Okay look…" I hesitated, then blurted, "It may have been Annie. Those amulets aren't safe, Jackson. I'm sure she was doing what she thought was best."

"It's not like her to break into the police station and steal evidence. She could have talked to me you know."

"I'm surprised she didn't, to be honest." I felt bad for throwing her under the bus. "How goes it with the case against Weaver?" I asked, hoping to change the subject and ignore the guilt churning in my gut. It worked. Jackson heaved a sigh and I imagined him running his fingers through his hair. "While it looks open and shut, it just doesn't make sense." He told me.

"The murder weapon in the back of the truck?" I guessed. It had been bugging me too.

"Why leave it in the open like that? Knowing that the police would be coming to talk to you sooner rather than later? And with blood still on it?"

"You're right. If you were going for the whole hide it in plain sight thing, you'd clean the blood off first."

"Exactly. Weaver claims he's innocent, that she was dead when he got there. I tend to believe him, although he's been remanded into custody while we sort this out."

A knock at the door distracted me and I glanced up

to see Jenna standing outside. She waved and I hurried over to unlock the door. "Sorry," I said to Jackson, "Jenna's just arrived."

"Ah, a meeting of the murder club I assume?" He teased.

"Of course." I grinned.

"I'll be right down." Jackson had participated in our murder club meetings a time or two in the past so it was no real surprise that he'd decided to attend this meeting. Then I clapped a hand over my mouth. Shoot, I'd forgotten about Gran. She was still at Driz's place. I'd called a couple of times throughout the day and the two of them were having a ball, cooking up a storm in the kitchen by the sounds of things—plus Gran had created an entire wardrobe for Driz. I suspect it consisted mostly of tulle and sequins.

"Don't suppose you could swing by and pick up Gran and Archie? They're with Driz." I asked hopefully.

"Sure." He agreed. "I'll see you in a few."

Within twenty minutes the gang was assembled. Monica unswaddled herself from the long cotton scarf she'd used to protect herself from the damaging rays of the sun and slumped into the armchair furthest from the windows. With a snap of my fingers, I pulled all the blinds down, not only blocking the sun but prying eyes. Jackson had arrived with Gran and Archie, and to my surprise, Driz. I shot him a look, confused, he'd stressed that

Driz wasn't to leave Tiny's house...so why was he here?

"A supervised visit," Jackson told me, dropping a quick kiss on my cheek in greeting. "It may help his case with the Council if he has some friendships already established in Whitefall Cove, people who will vouch for him."

"Oh." I nodded. Made sense. And Driz's presence was clearly making Gran happy. She'd crafted a pair of denim overalls with a large red sequined heart on the front, and a rainbow stripe down one leg. Driz wore them without a shirt, the straps crisscrossing over his back, but the denim against his scales looked good and at least he was wearing something.

"Everyone, this is Driz," Gran announced proudly. "And he's a Brezath."

"A Brezath?" Jackson asked.

"Yeah," Gran nodded. "That's the type of demon he is. You were right, he's not a crossroads demon, and he's definitely not a threat. Brezath's are quite domesticated and peaceful creatures—despite their appearance. Driz and I talked about all sorts of things today, his homeworld, and species being one of them."

"Why didn't you tell us you were a Brezath demon?" Jackson turned to Driz, who hunched one shoulder. "You didn't ask. Is it customary for you to introduce yourself as your species?"

I bit my lip to hold back a laugh. Fair point. "It's

fine, Driz." I told the demon. "You're right, we should have asked. So let's quickly rectify that. Gran and I are witches," I pointed to Monica. "Monica is a vampire, Jenna is a Fae, and Jackson here is a necromancer. And Archie," I pointed to the armchair next to the fireplace where Archie had curled up. "Is my familiar."

Gran grinned. "Now that we've got that out the way, is it time to call the murder club to order?"

FOURTEEN

Revealing the murder board with a wave of magic I stood studying it. A lot had changed since we'd put it together last night. For one, Glen Weaver had been arrested for Tiny's murder. I tapped the post-it note with Glen's name, drawing everyone's attention. "As I'm sure you're all aware, for Whitefall Cove has been talking about nothing else all day," I said, "Weaver was arrested last night."

"But we don't think he did it." Monica jumped in.

Jackson inclined his head. "Monica's right." He said. "While Weaver did return to Tiny's Garage—to try and convince her to let him have his truck back while he paid off his debt to her—she was already dead when he got there. Rather than call it in, he panicked, took his truck, closed up the Garage, and left. His prints are on the office door and the roller doors but not on the hoist, the vehicle Tiny was working on, or the murder weapon in the back of his truck."

"He wouldn't have been crazy enough to put on gloves for the murder and then take them off while still on the scene," Jenna commented, typing notes into her phone.

"So that metal pole was the murder weapon?" Monica asked.

"ME confirms it." Jackson nodded.

"The killer either hid the murder weapon in the back of Weaver's truck after killing Tiny, or they planted it later," I said, staring up at the ceiling as I visualized Tiny's Garage in my mind. "Weaver turning up presented him as the perfect fall guy. They could have followed him out to the fox's compound and planted the evidence."

"Which means they were there when Weaver turned up," Jackson said. "Could even have been in the garage, hiding."

"You don't think they hid the murder weapon?" I asked.

Jackson shook his head. "You said it yourself, Weaver's truck was covered in a tarp. Why waste precious moments getting under the tarp to place the murder weapon in the bed of the truck? It makes no sense. Way too risky. It would be easier to take it with you, clean it up, and dump it. There was no reason for the murder weapon to ever be found. Unless you were going to use it to frame someone else."

I struck off Glen Weaver's name and tapped the next one on the murder board. "Roxanne Mann. How did you go with her, Jenna?"

"Yeah good, I found out why she was at the garage and it's as you suspected Harper, nothing to do with getting her car serviced." Quickly scrolling through her phone Jenna continued. "Roxanne's fiancé, Carson, is sponsoring the Full Throttle Formula Masters race. There's a big social event coming up that they wanted Tiny to attend—along with her trophies—to help promote the race."

"Why would they want Tiny to attend?" Monica asked.

"Roxanne said that Jessie Mathis told her Tiny was returning to the racing scene as head mechanic for his team."

I glanced at Driz who was calmly watching proceedings. "She hadn't signed the contract though." I pointed out. "In fact, from what I overheard in her phone conversation with Mathis, she'd changed her mind. She wasn't going to join Mathis's team nor leave Whitefall Cove after all."

"That is correct." Driz nodded.

"Roxanne didn't mention any of that, just that Mathis told her Tiny's history and that she could be a good drawcard for the event. But when Roxanne invited her, Tiny demanded a five thousand dollar appearance fee."

Monica whistled. "Five k? That's pretty steep."

"Probably because she had no intention of actually attending." Gran sniffed. "Tiny liked to mess with people. Rather than saying no outright, or setting Roxanne straight, she'd have demanded an exorbitant fee and basically led Roxanne on. That's exactly the type of thing Tiny was known for. Sorry, Driz, no offense."

"None taken," Driz assured us. "I am well aware of Tiny's failings. But she wasn't like that with me—I saw a different side to her than what she shared with the rest of your charming town. But I could see that she did hold on to grudges. If you ever did her wrong, she would never forget. Nor forgive."

My mind went to the cash tin in Tiny's office, the one practically overflowing with cash. "Did Roxanne pay the fee?"

Jenna nodded. "Actually, she did."

"Don't tell me. In cash."

"Tiny demanded it," Jenna confirmed.

"Would you really pay a mechanic five thousand dollars to turn up to some fancy event promoting a car race?" Monica asked. "It's not like Tiny is a celebrity. Nor very...presentable." Another side-eye glance at Driz, who remained calm and amicable as we discussed his dearly departed love.

"She left the industry under a cloud that's for sure," I said. "Her team basically blacklisted her, preventing her from getting a position with another team."

"That's probably why she asked for five grand," Gran muttered. "To teach them buttholes a lesson."

We lapsed into silence, each lost in our own thoughts. Everything was connected but I was no closer to discovering the killer. They all had motive, except for Roxanne Mann. Why would she kill Tiny after paying her five thousand dollars to turn up to a car racing event? It made no sense. And did Tiny ask for cash just to inconvenience her? What had Tiny's plan been after accepting the cash? Did she intend to go to the event after all, or dishonor the agreement and keep the cash regardless?

Monica rolled her shoulders and approached the board. "You're forgetting something." She said. "The amulets. Someone distributed the amulets, someone has a deal with a crossroads demon." She turned to Jackson. "The fox who died, Del. Can you tell us what happened to him?"

"There's not much to tell. Preliminary autopsy results show his heart simply stopped beating. No blockages, no heart attack, it simply...stopped."

"So he wasn't crushed beneath the tractor?" I asked.

"Well his body was trapped beneath it, yes, but he

was dead before it happened. He died behind the wheel, the tractor was still in motion and basically it crashed and tipped."

Gran was nodding. "That's exactly how the Astrudian Amulet's work. Your soul is snatched with no outward sign of injury. Which is why it's so odd you found an amulet on Tiny's body."

"I see where you're going with this." Jackson crossed his arms. "Tiny was clearly murdered. If it was as a result of the amulet, she'd just be dead on the floor, no apparent injuries. And no need to make it look like an accident. Which reminds me, I'm going to need those amulets back, they're evidence."

Gran crossed her arms over her chest and rocked on her heels. "I don't have them. I thought you did?"

Jackson frowned. "No. They were stolen from the evidence lock-up."

Gran stiffened. "What? When?"

"You mean it wasn't you and Annie?" I gasped. I'd been sure it was Annie who'd liberated the coins.

"No, it wasn't me or Annie." She sighed, running a hand around the back of her neck. "Annie and I figured they were relatively safe at the cop shop, you all wear gloves when handling evidence, right?"

"Correct." Jackson acknowledged.

"The risk was minimal." Gran's forehead puckered. "So, what you're telling me is that now we have two Astrudian Amulet's back in play?"

"It looks that way." Jackson shot a worried look my way. I'd been the intended target for one of those amulets, but now I was aware of what they were and what they could do, I wouldn't be foolish enough to touch one. But if you didn't know, if you were presented with one, you'd naturally pick it up. Look at it. Touch it.

"Do you think the coins are related to Tiny's murder?" I asked.

"Where did you find the coin on Tiny?" Gran cut in. "Was it against her skin?"

"It was in her bra."

"Damn. So even if she'd picked it up with a rag, or had gloves on or whatever, as soon as she tucked it in her bra, as soon as it came into contact with her skin, it would have activated." Gran said.

"Which means it was planted on her after she'd died," Monica announced.

"Oh goody, the murder club is in session, guys you should have told me!" The ghost of Whitney Sims appeared, floating across the room to examine the murder board. Archie lifted his head, gave a half-hearted meow, and went back to sleep.

Whitney's gaze landed on Driz and she let out a blood-curdling scream before shooting up through the roof and off into the night. Driz blinked. "Well, that was unexpected."

My lips twitched and I tried to hold back the

laughter but then I saw Jackson's shoulders shaking as he too tried to control his mirth and it was too much, I burst into laughter. Before long the entire room was in hysterics, tears ran down my cheeks and I struggled to catch my breath. Gran slung an arm around my shoulders. "Let's continue this at Brewed Awakening, maybe a drink or two will loosen our brain cells so we can figure out whodunnit."

Numbers and figures danced before my eyes, blurring into one ineligible mess on the page. Flopping back in my seat I dug my knuckles into my eye sockets.

"You need to take a break," Driz announced, placing a mug of steaming coffee and a slice of pecan pie by my elbow. "You've been at this for hours."

Picking up the fork that accompanied the pie, I scooped up a piece and stuffed it into my mouth. "I know," I replied, mouth full. "But something has to be here. Something we're missing." I'd been painstakingly going through Tiny's accounts. She wasn't one for computers, however, she did keep a very detailed ledger but it was slow going.

My phone buzzed. Jackson was calling.

"Anything new?" I asked, cutting off another piece of pie.

"Good morning to you too." He drawled, voice warm in my ear.

"Sorry. Good morning."

"You sound tired. Didn't sleep well?" His concern was appreciated but I knew he wasn't going to like what was coming next.

"Actually...I'm at Tiny's. I guess I should call it Driz's now." I shot the demon a glance out the corner of my eye. He was hovering, I assumed he was waiting for me to finish my pie so he could whisk away the plate and wash up. He was incredibly attentive that way. "I've been going through Tiny's accounts from the garage."

"We have forensics to do that." Jackson pointed out.

"Yes, I know, but..." I didn't know how to explain to him how a strangely desperate need burned through me to solve Tiny's murder. Unlike the other cases I'd been involved in, this one held no particular personal connection to me, so I was puzzled myself as to why it was so important, why I felt so driven.

"I think I know what the problem is."

"Oh?" Good. At least someone knew what the hell was going on, for I just couldn't figure it out. Who had killed Tiny? And why? I was no closer to solving the puzzle than I had been when we'd found her body.

"You're using this as a distraction."

What? I blinked, pulled the phone from my ear to stare at it before replying. "Distraction? From what?"

"The Garrag attack." He prompted.

"Tiny's murder kinda trumped everything."

"Including your birthday."

I frowned. "Well yeah, but that's okay. We'll celebrate later, that doesn't worry me." Plus, it had been Tiny's birthday too and she'd ended up dead. Hard to really want to celebrate your own special day after that.

"Harper, it's been a hellish few days. You were attacked, an Astrudian Amulet was left for you, then Tiny's murder. It's okay to take a step back on this one, you don't have to solve every little mystery that befalls Whitefall Cove."

I blew out a breath, running a hand around the back of my neck. He was right. I'd thrown myself headlong into investigating Tiny's murder because I didn't want to think about the one thing that had me really rattled. Why had the Garrag attacked? Why now, after all this time? And why me? "I hate it when you're right," I grumbled into the phone. But there was something else I hadn't told him. My talk with Annie. The very real possibility that I just might get the boot from the coven.

"Harper?" Jackson's voice on the end of the line reminded me he was still there.

"Yeah, look, something else happened on my

birthday. Well not really happened, just…something was said to me, and it rattled me."

"Said? By whom? And what did they say?" I could hear the protectiveness in his voice, like he was rolling up his sleeves and preparing to go beat the living snot out of anyone who said anything to upset me.

"It was Annie," I admitted. "Annie is, as you know, the head witch of the Sisters of the Sacred Flame Coven."

"Is this about the amulets?" Jackson asked.

I shook my head. "No. It's about me. And my witch responsibilities."

"Okaaaaay…"

I sighed. "Basically she's mad at me, says I haven't been pulling my weight as a witch, that I've blown off the last three coven meetings and that she has concerns over my suitability to be a member of the coven."

There was a seconds pause. "Harsh." He finally said. "How do you feel about that?"

"Gutted." I admitted. "And scared. Scared she's going to kick me out."

"But? That sentence sounded like there was a but on the end."

"But she has a point. I have been…coasting, I guess you'd call it. And I didn't think the coven meetings were that important."

"What does Gran say?"

"Not much. We talked about it briefly in passing but I think I need to sit down and talk it out with her. I guess finding out I was a whitelight witch and having all this power kinda went to my head and that maybe I didn't need the coven?" It was the first time I'd admitted such a thing out loud. But now I was presented with the very real danger of being kicked out of the coven, I realized how much I needed them. Annie was right. Coven was family.

Red really was my color. I watched as the manicurist deftly painted my nails—she made it look so easy, every steady stroke covering my nail in crimson. Whenever I attempted to do it myself at home I ended up painting half my finger along with my nail. I'd given in to Jackson's coaxing to take a break. Wendy was looking after the store, Driz was content baking at home, I could afford to sit and have my nails done.

"Purple suits me don't you think?" Gran asked, waving her hand in my face to show me her own manicure.

"Sure, Gran looks great." I smiled absently. Today's outfit was black fishnet stockings beneath black metallic hot-pants, a leather corset with a whole lot of buckles and chains on the front, cinched tight over a purple T-shirt. On her feet, fluffy black Ugg boots. Massive hoop earrings dangled from her earlobes, and at least twenty bracelets, all black or silver, some with spikes, some without, stretched along one forearm almost to her elbow.

"What's up with you?" She peered at me through eyes heavily rimmed with black eyeliner. I smirked a little at the sight. She actually resembled a raccoon more than a badass biker chic. Of course, I was smart enough not to tell her that.

"Nothing." Truth be told I'd been trying to throw off the funk I was currently in and had let Jackson talk me into a trip to the nail salon but so far I hadn't been able to stop thinking about Tiny's death. I'd found two strange entries in her accounts that puzzled me. Two deposits, both for five thousand dollars, months apart. No record of what they were for or where they came from. Did Tiny have a habit of charging five thousand dollar appearance fees? I hadn't thought she'd be in that much demand, but then I didn't move in racing circles—but if the money had come from event organizers, why hadn't she documented it? I raised my hand toward my mouth to chew a nail when the technician grabbed my wrist and squeezed it. Hard.

"None of that! You'll ruin my work." Turning on a small fan sitting on the table, she directed me to hold my wet nails in front of it. "Sit here until they're dry." She instructed. "No touching."

"Got it." I nodded, taken aback by her ferocity. I guess she took her work seriously. Sitting there with my nails drying a strange smell wafted my way. I sniffed, then coughed. Urgh, it was vile.

"Gran? Was that you?" I choked, my eyes starting to water.

"What, love?" She turned toward me and as she did so ever so subtly lifted one butt cheek and released another stinker.

I coughed. "God! What did you eat?"

She fluttered her fake eyelashes at me. "I don't know what you mean, Harper Jones." The next fart was audible and I barked out a laugh. The nail technician who'd been busy putting away the varnish we'd chosen paused and lifted her nose, sniffing the air. With a muttered curse she hurried to the front door and pinned it open, shooting Gran an accusing glare.

"Busted," I whispered out the corner of my mouth.

"So anyway," Gran leaned toward me, "I was next door at Curl Up & Dye before you called suggesting a nail date, when I overheard Kathleen Griffin and Pamela Moss having a good old gossip session while having their greys done."

"Jacob and Sarah's moms'?"

"That's them. Sitting there with their heads covered in foil, chatting up a storm."

I waved a hand, careful not to smear my polish. "Okay. So what?"

Gran leaned even closer. "Well, they were talking about Roxanne Mann for starters." She said smugly.

Now that got my attention. I grinned conspiratorially. "Do tell."

"Well," Gran glanced around as if to make sure no-one was listening, then leaned even closer. If she leaned any further she'd topple off her chair. "Both women were behind her at the ATM, at different times, when she withdrew a lot of cash. The limit you can withdraw at the machine."

I frowned. "Five thousand?" That number kept coming up. Gran nodded. "Sure, if that's the limit."

"So they each saw her withdraw five thousand dollars. At different times. When was this?"

"Kathleen said she saw her about three months ago, and Pamela said it was ages ago, more like six months."

So roughly every quarter Roxanne was withdrawing large amounts of cash. The question was...why? "Why were they talking about Roxanne anyway?" I asked, already lifting my hand toward my mouth again when I remembered the manicurist's stern words and quickly shoved my nails in front of the fan to continue drying.

"They were talking about everyone, darl. Who was wearing what, who's shagging who—nothing new to report there, sadly—of course, Roxanne came up because she was wearing that Carla Zampatti jumpsuit and everyone was green with envy."

"The navy one with the gold floral print?" I remembered seeing her in it too. No wonder people were talking, it was a stunning outfit.

"That's the one. Of course, you can get knock offs that look similar, but the one Roxanne was wearing was pure silk."

I whistled. "Expensive."

Gran snorted. "Of course. Nothing but the best for Roxanne. And that was what everyone was talking about. How she came into money."

"How did she?"

"Well, most of it comes from Carson Singh. Smart girl, hitching herself to a rich guy."

"But what do we know about her, besides she's going to marry Carson, who's Whitefall Cove's richest man?" And it niggled at me. Why did Roxanne go to Tiny's garage? Why invite Tiny personally, why not send the event organizer or assistant or whatever. We knew Roxanne and Carson had a bevy of people who were paid to help run their lives. It didn't make sense to me that someone who wears designer silk and Jimmy Choo's would visit Tiny in her garage.

"There's something more to this," I said, more to myself than to Gran, but she answered anyway.

"And why would Miss Moneybags need cash?

She's got credit cards out the wazoo. The only time you use cash is when you don't want it traced. Now, I admit, initially, I thought maybe she was a fraud, maybe her designer threads were knock offs and she was paying some woman to whip up an outfit in her spare bedroom and paid her in untraceable cash, but on closer inspection, I realize I was wrong. Those clothes are the real deal."

And then it all started slotting into place, like pieces of a puzzle. The withdrawn cash. Tiny's undocumented deposits. It couldn't be a coincidence that Roxanne withdrew the cash and Tiny deposited it. My heart rate spiked as a shot of adrenaline raced through me. Roxanne Mann was paying that money to Tiny. And the only conclusion I could draw? Blackmail.

As soon as the manicurist decreed my nails were dry, I was out the door, pulling my phone out of my bag as I went.

"Wait up!" Gran called, hurrying after me. "What's got your panties in a wad?"

"What?" I glanced down at her. "Nothing. I just had a thought, that's all."

"About Roxanne?" Gran guessed.

"Exactly. I think maybe Tiny was blackmailing her. And that's why Roxanne was withdrawing cash. There are three unexplained deposits in Tiny's account."

"Hmmm. So what could our giant, bad-tempered, not very liked fairy possibly have over Miss.

Moneybags?" Gran tapped her purple lips with her purple-tipped fingers. "Sex?"

My eyes widened. "Maybe Tiny caught Roxanne in a compromising position with someone other than her fiancée?"

Gran's lips pursed. "Could be."

"It's certainly something you wouldn't want getting out." I continued.

"But is it something you'd pay five thousand dollars to keep quiet?"

"Fifteen thousand." I corrected. "Three lots." I paused, Gran skidding to a halt beside me.

"What is it?" She asked.

"Roxanne told Jenna the five thousand was an appearance fee."

"Yeah? So?"

"So I know one way to find out if that was the truth or a lie."

Gran grinned. "Are you thinking what I'm thinking?"

I snorted. "Probably not! But go ahead."

"I'm thinking we crash the big event that Tiny was paid to attend."

I looked at Gran in surprise. That was exactly what I was thinking. "I'm going to call Jenna, I bet she can swing us an invite, the paper must be covering it." I dialed. Jenna picked up on the first ring.

"Can you get us into the Full Throttle Formula Masters Fundraiser event?" I asked without preamble.

"Of course." She replied instantly. "I'm not covering it, Jeremy is, but I can get us tickets. How many?"

I glanced at Gran. "Do you want to come?"

"Snort. Of course! And don't forget Monica."

"Four tickets," I replied. "You, me, Gran, and Monica."

"Jackson?"

"Better make that five. He may be working but we'll get him a ticket just in case."

"You do realize it's tonight, right?"

I hadn't, but no matter, it was doable. After all, Gran and I had just had our nails done, be a shame to waste them. "That's fine. Are you still in the office?"

"Yep. What else do you need?"

"Can you run a background check on Roxanne Mann?" I dropped my voice. "I think Tiny may have been blackmailing her. But I've got nothing to back that up, just a hunch and a sorta-kinda money trail."

"Cash?" Jenna guessed.

"Exactly."

"Difficult to trace." She agreed. "I'll see what I can turn up. I'll see you tonight at the fundraiser and fill you in on what I find. I'll have your tickets left at the door."

"Fantastic. Thanks, Jenna, you're a gem."

As soon as I disconnected the call my phone beeped with an incoming text. So did Grans. Opening the message I sighed. "A coven meeting?" I asked incredulously.

"Looks that way," Gran said, dropping her phone back into her bag.

"But Gran, we can't go. We've got the fundraising event. I need to get to the bottom of whatever Roxanne Mann is hiding."

A myriad of emotions crossed Gran's face. Speculation, concern, disappointment, I read them all. My heart fell. This was exactly what Annie meant. I put everything else in front of the coven. And something told me if I blew them off tonight, I'd be turning my back on them forever. Gran opened her mouth to speak but I held up my hand to silence her. "I know. I heard it as soon as it left my mouth. You're right. Of course, we're going to the coven meeting. We'll go to the fundraiser after. I'll text Jenna and Monica that we'll be late, they can suss it out before we get there."

Gran inclined her head. "Wise choice."

CHAPTER
SIXTEEN

Standing in the field behind Annie's house in heels was no easy feat, but I did it, despite pulling my stilettos out of the soil over a dozen times. We stood in a circle surrounding a fire, the flames leaping up into the sky. It was twilight, the sun had all but disappeared over the horizon casting shadows of purple and blue across the land.

"Glad you could make it." Annie nodded her head in my direction and a flush crawled up my neck to heat my cheeks at her dig. I inclined my head in return but refrained from answering. After all, what could I say in my defense? That I'd been too busy in the past to bother turning up?

We held hands while Annie cast the circle, thanking the Goddess, the earth, wind, fire, and water.

The shape of a pentagram flared up in the flames before disappearing as quickly as it had appeared.

"Sisters of the Sacred Flame, we are at a crossroads," Annie said. I cast a surprised look around the circle. We weren't a big coven, beside me and Gran there was Annie, head witch, then Agnes, Jennifer, and Leah.

"What's up?" Gran asked.

"I won't keep you long." Annie looked from me in my red evening gown, the one I'd bought for my birthday date with Jackson, and Gran who was in a purple tutu, fishnet stockings, and a black barely there bustier. "I can see you ladies have plans."

"You're burning daylight here, Annie." Gran pointed out. I squeezed her hand in warning. Don't antagonize the head witch. If there was a rule book for our coven, that should be the number one rule. But then Gran had never been much for rules.

"Hardly." Annie winked at me and I relaxed somewhat. Perhaps I'd made some ground in redeeming myself by showing up tonight. Again, guilt ate at me that I'd let them down. It had never been my intention, I'd just been...busy.

Annie cleared her throat. "The time has come for me to retire." She announced.

"Retire?" Agnes squawked. "Witches don't retire. They die."

We all looked at Annie in horror. Was she dying?

Oh my God, now I felt even worse about blowing her off. She waved a hand, calming us. "Relax. I've no intention of dying. But I do have plans and leading the Sisters of the Sacred Flame is impeding those plans."

Gran turned to me and stage whispered, "She's got a fella. She wants to shag his socks off I bet."

"Ssh," I whispered back. I didn't think that was Annie's reason for retiring. You didn't need to retire to have sex—Gran was proof of that.

"Can we ask?" Leah piped up.

Annie grinned. "Sure! I want to travel. I want to see the world. In all my three hundred years on this planet, I've seen very little of it. And now that I've found a replacement, I'd rather she take over now, rather than wait until I die before she takes the reins."

We all looked at Gran, who was second in charge of our coven, fully expecting her to step up into the role of head witch, but Gran surprised us all by shaking her finger at us. "Oh no! It ain't me. I don't want the gig, talk about long term commitment. Pft."

"Who then?" Agnes asked. I could tell by the way she was preening that she thought it would be her. After all, if you were going to choose the head of the coven based on age, she'd be next in line at seventy-two.

"Harper." Annie announced.

"What?" I gasped, clutching a hand to my throat.

Leah grabbed my arm, grinning, "You'd be perfect, Harper! Oh congratulations, this is wonderful news!"

I frowned down at Gran who was jumping up and down. "Did you know about this?" I accused. I didn't know what to think. Leading up to this moment I thought I was in danger of being turfed out of the coven, now I was being handed the reins? I wasn't sure if I wanted the honor.

Annie caught my attention across the dancing firelight. "You passed all the tests." She told me. "Plus as a whitelight witch, the coven couldn't be in better hands."

"Tests?" I narrowed my eyes. She hadn't turned the Garrag loose on me had she, to prove I was capable? Because I'd failed that particular test in quite a spectacular fashion.

"Oh relax, it's nothing nefarious. You really do have a suspicious mind." She scolded. "I've been monitoring your progress since your return to Whitefall Cove and the coven. You've shown yourself to be dedicated to the town and townsfolk. You've continued to embrace and learn the power of your magic, despite countless hurdles. You're not one hundred percent there yet but I'm confident you will become the witch our ancestors envisioned."

"Get back to this test," I grumbled, not liking that she'd been testing me without my knowledge. Gran gave me a nudge in the ribs but I ignored her. Annie continued. "It was very simple. All you had to do was turn up tonight. And you did."

I almost sagged with relief. Her test had been basic. Chew me out for non-attendance then call an unexpected and highly inconvenient coven meeting. Game well played Annie Robins. I considered what she'd just told me. "But you just said I'm not one hundred percent ready yet?"

Annie sobered. "Correct. You're not. I am going to groom you to take over. By the end of the year, you will be the head witch of the Sisters of the Sacred Flame Coven. And you'd better be ready because I've got a cruise booked in January and I have no intention of canceling it." She sniffed. "Now normally we'd celebrate at this point in time, however, I know Harper and Alice have plans this evening, not to mention the murder club is in hot pursuit of Tiny's killer. We'll hold off any celebrations until Harper officially takes the wheel. Anyone got an issue with that?"

It seems the coven was in agreement. I was to be the next head witch. Annie closed the circle, killed the flames and we began to disburse, picking our way across the field. I was shocked into silence, not knowing what to think at this turn of events. Never in a million years did I expect Annie to announce she was retiring and handing the coven over to me, of all people. I snuck a glance at Agnes, who'd stiffened when Annie had made the announcement, and despite offering words of congratulations, I could see the hurt in her eyes.

"Give her time," Gran said softly, linking her arm with mine.

"You always did know what I was thinking." I chuckled.

"Your face is an open book." She wasn't the only one to say that. I wondered if that was something Annie would have me work on, during our hand-over phase?

Reaching my car I stopped and waved a handful of magic over us, eliminating the dirt from our shoes before we climbed in the car. I sat behind the wheel, eyes staring unseeingly out of the windscreen.

"Gran...I'm not sure I want this," I whispered.

Gran snorted. "You were made for this, Harper Jones. This is your destiny. You just can't see it yet. You got yourself all muddled when you left Whitefall Cove and decided to live as a human. I wish I'd had the foresight to stop you then. A witch turning her back on magic is never a good idea."

"But what if I'm no good at it?" I protested.

"Girl, you are going to be amazingly brilliant at it. You're going to take to it like a duck to water."

It was my turn to snort. "How do you know?"

"Er, hello, I am a witch too you know. I might be old but I ain't lost my faculties yet." She clipped her seatbelt on and looked at me expectantly. "Well? Are we going to the ball, Cinderella? I've got me a hankering to give Carson Singh a turn around the dancefloor he'll never forget."

The Full Throttle Formula Masters Fundraiser was in full swing when we arrived. Black and white checkered banners decorated the walls of the Town Hall, tall round tables made to look like stacked car tires dotted the room, and waiters dressed in racing suits continually moved around the room with trays of champagne and canapes.

I snagged a glass of champagne just as Jenna came rushing up. "Oh good, you're here." She had her phone clasped in one hand and an empty glass in the other. "I spotted Jodie Bell a second ago, have you talked to her yet?"

Jodie Bell was the owner of the yellow car that Tiny had been working on. "No, I haven't. No time like the present." I hooked an arm through Jenna's. "Lead me to her."

Gran was long gone. As soon as we'd checked our coats at the door Gran was off in search of Carson Singh, seems she really did have a hankering to dance with the man. I wondered if I should seek him out and warn him?

"How did the coven thing go? It didn't take long, I

was expecting you to be gone for a couple of hours at least." Jenna said, weaving her way through the crowd of bodies, pulling me along with her.

"Yeah," I puffed out a breath. "Get this, Annie wants to retire and she wants me to take her place as head witch."

Jenna glanced at me, eyebrows raised. "Is that a good thing or a bad thing? I can't tell by your face if you're happy about it or not."

I bit my lip. "I honestly don't know. I thought I was on the brink of being booted out. To suddenly learn that I'm basically getting a promotion? I'm not sure I want the responsibility, to be honest."

"What does Gran say?"

"She says I was born for it."

"Well then." Jenna nodded as if it were a fait accompli. "There she is."

I spotted Jodie Bell talking with our Mayor, Elaine Burch. Jodie was a petite little thing, with bright red hair and a spatter of freckles across her nose and cheeks. She was in animated conversation with the Mayor, her hands waving, her drink in danger of spilling. Spotting us approaching, Mayor Burch smiled.

"Harper. Jenna. Good to see you here tonight." She greeted us.

"Great turnout," Jenna said. "Actually, I'm glad I

caught up with you, I was hoping to get a picture and a quote for the paper?"

Mayor Burch smiled and placed her glass on the table she and Jodie had been standing next to. "Absolutely. Where do you want me?"

Jenna pointed to the stage that was decorated to resemble a finishing line. "I think up there would be great?" She threw me a wink as she ushered the Mayor away.

I smiled at Jodie. "How are you, Jodie? Terrible business about Tiny."

She shuddered and took a sip of her drink. "It sure was. I heard you were the one who found her? That must have been so awful."

"It was. I know Tiny wasn't the easiest person to get on with, but she didn't deserve what happened to her."

A half-smile flitted across Jodi's face. "You know, I'd heard that about Tiny—that she was...difficult. But I didn't have a problem with her."

"You must be a minority." I snorted. I glanced around the room. "Pretty sure Tiny has had words with almost everyone here at one time or another."

"The trick to staying on Tiny's good side was pretty simple."

"Oh?"

"Pay her in advance. Money talks. If there's

anything I've learned from working for the Singh Corporation, it's that."

I blinked in surprise. "You work for Carson Singh?" I hadn't known that.

"I work for the Singh Corporation." She corrected me. "I'm not one of Carson's PAs or anything like that."

"So what do you do?" A waiter drifted by carrying a tray of something smelling delicious. I waved him over. "What do we have here?" I asked, indicating the tray.

"Mozzarella toasts with spicy herb oil." He replied, offering me a napkin. I piled up three of the small triangles of toast onto the napkin and thanked him. Jodie declined and waved him away.

"Sorry," I apologized to her. "I'm starving."

"I can see that." She grinned. "I'm the event coordinator for the Singh Corporation. I'm responsible for all of this."

"Even the mozzarella toasts?" I mumbled around a mouthful of the most delicious toast I'd had in my entire life.

Jodie was nodding. "Even the toasts."

"So working for the Singh Corporation would come with some perks, surely?"

"What, besides a very attractive salary, medical, and leave package?" She eyed me speculatively.

"Well, I was thinking about your car actually."

"My car?" Her eyebrows shot up in surprise.

"Yeah, I know Carson has more than one car, I've seen him driving around town in several different vehicles, so I imagine he has some sort of fleet."

"He does, but I don't have a company vehicle if that's what you're getting at."

"No, no, I was just thinking that because he has a fleet, he'd have a pretty sweet deal with a mechanic for regular servicing and repairs. I'd have thought you could swing an employee discount for your car there. Why take it to Tiny's?"

"That's easy. Tiny was the best mechanic there was. Hands down. I would happily have paid double to take my car to her."

It was my turn to blink in surprise. "I'd heard that Tiny was good but was she really that good? I mean, her garage is a mess, she's easily irritated, she has the most creative accounting system I've ever seen..." I trailed off.

"Had. She had all of those things." Jodie corrected, green eyes intent as she studied me.

"Yes. Had." I cleared my throat. "How long had Tiny had your car for?"

Jodie rolled one shoulder in a shrug. "I dropped it in the night before. Tiny liked to get an early start. She said she'd need it for a couple of days."

"I'm curious about something. Since you were getting your car serviced at the time, why didn't you give Tiny her invitation to this then?" I waved my hand, indicating the decorated room around us. "Why did Roxanne hand-deliver the invite?"

Jodie frowned. "I don't know what you're talking about. Tiny wasn't on the guest list."

Yeah. Just as I'd figured. Jodie continued, "We have to keep an eye on numbers, due to restrictions with hiring the hall. After the official guest list is sorted and we've got our confirmations, then we know how many tickets we can sell."

"And that was part of your job? As event coordinator, to oversee the guest list and ticket sales?"

"Of course! The guest list is reserved for VIPs, and as much as Tiny was a great mechanic, she wasn't a VIP. VIPs are those with deep pockets who understand the importance of bringing along their checkbooks. Tiny has never—as far as I'm aware—donated anything to any other business in town. Like I said, she could have bought a ticket if she wanted to attend. Or someone could buy a ticket for her, either way." She ended on a shrug. Her eyes narrowed and focused on something over my shoulder. "If you'll excuse me?" She hurried away before I could respond.

"Well?" Jenna was back. She must have been watching my exchange with Jodie and swooped in as soon as the other woman had left.

"Another fan of Tiny's mechanical skills." I sipped my champagne, casting an eye around the room for another waiter with a tray of food. "She's responsible for all of this." I said, waving the hand with my champagne glass to indicate the decor around us. "She's the event coordinator for the Singh Cooperation."

"She's done a brilliant job." Jenna nodded her head in approval. "This place looks amazing."

"It also means she was in charge of the guest list and ticket sales, and Tiny was not invited. Not officially." I snagged a spring roll from a passing waiter, shoving it into my mouth.

"We already know—or at least suspect very strongly—that the five thousand dollar appearance fee wasn't an appearance fee at all, but blackmail money." Jenna reminded me.

"Well, this confirms it. Jodie organized the entire event. She would have mentioned that they'd paid Tiny five thousand dollars to turn up. She also said Tiny wasn't VIP material, that those guests are the ones who donate large sums of money to events like these."

"Makes sense." Jenna agreed. "Tiny was tight with her money for sure. She never bought raffle tickets, never supported charities. She wasn't a community-oriented person."

I raised a finger to my mouth to chew a nail but then remembered my beautifully manicured nails and quickly snatched my hand away. "I need to have a chat with Roxanne," I muttered, searching through the crowd for the other woman. I didn't see her, but I did catch a glimpse of non-other than Jessie Mathis. I wasn't into the whole racing scene, but I did recognize his photos from the covers of magazines in Tiny's workshop.

I turned and grabbed Jenna's wrist, dragging her after me as I made my way toward the racing car driver. "There's Mathis," I told her. "Let's go talk to him. He was in negotiations with Tiny for her to join his team."

Jessie Mathis was a good looking man. Tall, with an athletic build, a dusting of a five o'clock shadow on a strong jaw. I was not surprised to find Gran hanging off his arm.

"I thought you wanted to dance with Carson?" I asked as we approached. Gran winked. "I'll get to Carson, don't you worry. In the meantime, I found this lovely stud." She slapped her palm on Jessie's rear, making him jump. God, she was going to get sued for sexual harassment one of these days.

"Sorry." I offered up in way of a very weak apology. Jessie Mathis eyed me up and down, the gleam in his eyes telling me he liked what he saw. I stiffened. I'd never been a fan of sexual objectification but then I didn't have room for complaint when my own grandmother was doing that very thing to him.

"She's quite a woman." Jessie smiled, his ultra white teeth dazzling in the extreme. "She yours?"

"She's my grandmother." I offered a weak smile.

"And you are?"

"This is my granddaughter, Harper Jones. Harper goes out with our local detective, Jackson Ward." Gran piped up, making it clear to Jessie that I wasn't available. I darted her a grateful look. There was a general air of confidence around Jessie Mathis that told me he was used to pulling the ladies, that he was bathed in female adoration everywhere he went. I couldn't deny he was a good looking man, and rich to boot—he clearly ticked all the boxes for Gran!

"I hear you were in negotiations with Tiny for her to join your team as head mechanic." I smiled politely.

"Yeah? Where did you hear that?" He leaned one elbow on the tall cocktail table by his side and crossed his ankles.

"I saw a copy of the contract."

"Is that right?"

Hmmm. He wasn't the chatty type, but the way his eyes were lingering on my cleavage told me it wasn't talking that he was interested in. Before I could say anything, Gran smacked his arm. Hard. "Her eyes are up there." Gran did the two-finger point thing, indicating Jessie should remove his gaze from my chest and look me in the eye. To my utter amusement, he blushed.

"Any reason why Tiny didn't sign it?" I decided to ignore the whole ogling thing.

His sigh was big and heartfelt. "She was going to. When I first approached her she was keen. Head mechanic. Big salary. More than she'd make at that garage of hers."

"But it meant what? Leaving town? A lot of travel?"

"Yeah, I needed her on the circuit. Not feasible for her to run her garage and be head mechanic, so she'd have to either sell up or bring in a manager."

"So you weren't forcing her to close down?"

He snorted. "Why would I do that? I don't care if she had a side business or ten, I just needed her to be on the circuit with me."

"Why's that so important?"

"I'm having another run at the Daytona 500. It's the season-opening race in Florida and I wanted my Mustang on that track and in top shape. I aim to win."

"But you guys blackballed Tiny. Forced her out of the racing industry. Why would she come back?"

"All of that was before my time. All I know is that she's a top-notch mechanic. And she has no family ties. That's perfect for this life. No distractions, no hankering to get back home to the significant other or kids or whatever. Aside from her garage, she had no commitments. To be honest I thought it would be an easy sell. And it was to start with, then negotiations stalled..."

That must have been when Driz turned up. "Did she say why? Why she'd changed her mind?"

He shook his head. "If you knew Tiny at all you'd know she doesn't give reasons or excuses. She does what she wants. She just said she was no longer interested."

"Yet you kept calling her," I recalled the conversation I overheard in Tiny's bathroom.

One shoulder hunched. "Figured I could try and wear her down. But I had feelers out for another mechanic, knew I couldn't wait on Tiny for much longer."

"Right." He confirmed what I'd already surmised. He had no motive for wanting Tiny dead. "Where were you the day she died?" I just need to clear up one last thing.

"Me? You think I killed her?" He straightened, face alarmed.

"Actually, I don't. But I need to cross you off my list."

"Your list?"

"Harper is an amateur detective." Gran piped up, chest puffed out with pride. "She's been instrumental in helping solve several murders in Whitefall Cove."

"Gran," I warned. She made it sound like people were being killed left right and center, and that wasn't actually the case, but still, it didn't sound good when you said it like that.

"Is that right?" Jessie eyed me speculatively. "Well in that case, happy to oblige. I was in Florida actually. At the Daytona International Speedway. We were taking the Mustang for a test drive on the track. My team was with me—they can confirm. Does that get me off your list?"

"Thank you for your cooperation."

SEVENTEEN

Carson Singh was tall, dark, and handsome. Not to mention rich, and one hundred percent human. And I admit, I was a teeny bit starstruck when I somehow found myself in his arms on the dance floor. I'd been heading toward Gran, who'd abandoned Mathis in favor of Carson and had managed to drag the millionaire out onto the dance floor. Bless him for not being a rude jerk and actually pandering to my eccentric Gran's whims. But as soon as Gran saw me approaching, she'd claimed to need a bathroom break and practically thrust Carson at me, asking me if I'd mind her spot.

"I'm sorry about my Gran." I felt compelled to apologize. Carson chuckled. "It's perfectly alright. She's quite the character."

"She sure is." I breathed in his scent. Whatever cologne he was wearing was quite delicious and if I didn't know that he was human I'd have sworn he was using some sort of spell on me. Despite being madly in love with Jackson, I wasn't immune to the man's allure. He was drop-dead gorgeous and Roxanne Mann was one lucky lady.

"So, tell me, Carson," I leaned back slightly to look up into his face. "How did you and Roxanne meet?"

His smile was instant. "At an event much like this actually."

"Oh, a fundraiser? Here, in Whitefall Cove?"

"No, it was in the city. I was there on business. It was one of those big formal affairs. Tuxedos and ballgowns. And she walked in and I was pretty much lost as soon as I laid eyes on her. She was by far the most beautiful woman in the room."

"How sweet." I smiled. "Love at first sight." I wondered then if Roxanne were a witch. Maybe it was she who was casting spells. "Where is she by the way?" I asked. "I haven't seen her all night."

"Oh, she's around here somewhere." He glanced over my head as if searching for her in the crowd.

"Tell me about her." I invited. "I've only met her that time I bumped into her in Tiny's garage."

"Tiny's garage?" His eyebrows lowered. "What was she doing there?"

"Ummm. I'm not sure. She didn't say. I thought it was to invite Tiny to this, but Jodie told me Tiny wasn't on the VIP list."

Carson snorted. "She most definitely wasn't. All of our special guests have made contributions in five or six figures. Tiny hasn't managed two figures."

"Yeah, she wasn't one to open her checkbook." I had no idea these fundraisers attracted that much money, but then I moved in very different circles to Carson Singh.

"So, Carson," I smiled as we twirled around the dancefloor. "Is this whole car racing thing a personal interest of yours? Or is it all business?"

He chuckled. "A little of both. My hobby, well, it's pretty boring actually. Roxanne rolls her eyes whenever I start talking about it."

"Oh?" I prompted. "Do tell. What boring hobbies do millionaires have?"

"I'm into ancient artifacts." He smiled down at me. "I especially love anything Egyptian."

"Really?" I beamed. "My parents are archeologists! They're actually on an expedition—multiple expeditions really—in Australia."

"Wait! Harper Jones. Jones, as in Judith and Keith Jones?" Our dancing slowed to a halt as we looked at each in surprise.

"Yes. They're my parents."

His face lit up like a kid in a candy store. "Harper, I'm so pleased to meet you." He clasped one of my hands in both of his and shook it enthusiastically. "I follow your parents' journals and papers, they do magnificent work. I had no idea you were their daughter."

"Next time they're in town I'll introduce you." I offered, a little taken aback about his passion for archaeology and the change in his demeanor. Gone was the smooth debonair businessman and in his place an overenthusiastic artifact collector.

"Darling, there you are." The sultry tones of non-other than Roxanne Mann came from behind me. I slid my hand from Carson's and plastered a smile on my face as I turned to greet her.

"Roxanne," Carson slid an arm around her waist and dropped a kiss on her cheek. "Have you met Harper Jones? She's the daughter of Judith and Keith Jones. Archeologists." He'd dialed down his earlier excitement, but there was a twinkle in his eyes telling me he'd like nothing more than to talk my ear off about mom and dad's adventures.

She patted his arm and fluttered her eyelashes at him. "That's wonderful darling, but don't forget we have other guests. Let's not monopolize Miss Jones hmmm?"

Carson's face sobered and he shot a look my way.

"I'm sorry. I forget that not everyone is excited about old rocks as I am."

"Not at all. My parents are archeologists, how could I possibly find old rocks boring? Actually, I came across something myself the other day. Have you ever heard of an Astrudian Amulet?" I asked on the off chance that Carson may have heard of them, maybe even been offered them to purchase. Someone had stolen them from the police station. One of them had been used to reap Del's soul. Annie still had the one that had been left for me. And then there was the one that had been planted on Tiny's body.

One dark brow arched and he leaned closer. "No, I haven't, but I'm intrigued! Tell me more!"

Roxanne's nostrils flared and her dark eyes flashed. Looping her arm through Carson's she tugged. "Sweetheart, I promised Edgel Ottaway I'd return with you. He's our biggest contributor, we wouldn't want to disappoint him now would we?" While her voice was a purr, her eyes were shooting daggers at me.

"Right, yes, of course." Carson straightened. "Harper, can we continue this conversation another time? Maybe catch up for a coffee?"

My eyes darted from him to Roxanne and back again. She looked ready to explode. I smiled sweetly. "That would be lovely. I look forward to it."

Roxanne finally managed to drag him away. As soon as they were in the clear Jenna and Monica rushed up to me. "What was that all about? She looked furious! Were you making a play for Carson?" Monica drawled, nudging me in the ribs.

I snorted. "No. I'm taken, remember? But no, it turns out Carson has a thing for ancient artifacts, and he just realized who my parents are—he got very excited."

"We could tell. The two of you were very animated. I'm not surprised Roxanne swooped in and rushed to claim her man." Jenna teased.

"It wasn't like that." I protested, then when the two of them burst out laughing I realized they'd been teasing me. "Oh ha ha. But given his interest in artifacts and such, I asked him if he'd ever heard of an Astrudian Amulet."

"Had he?" Jenna asked.

"No. And he wanted to know more. But Roxanne looked like she was about to have a fit and dragged him away."

"So she either sees you as a threat," Monica said, eyeing me in my red gown. "Or...what? She doesn't want you telling him about the amulets?"

I sighed. I wasn't bothered what Roxanne thought of me one way or the other. "Also, he seemed very surprised that Roxanne was at Tiny's garage."

"She's in the middle of all of this," Jenna said.

"Agreed. I asked him to tell me about her but then we got distracted with other things. All I know is that they met at a black-tie event in the city. I think it's time we did some digging into her background." I said.

"And by we, you mean me." Jenna grinned. I wrapped an arm around her shoulders. "Of course, who else?"

"May I interrupt?" Jackson's warm breath against my ear had me spinning and launching myself into his arms. "You made it!"

"Yep. And it was totally worth it. You look amazing." After returning my embrace he held me at arm's length, taking a thorough inventory of my red, figure-hugging dress.

"You don't look so bad yourself." I grinned, admiring his black suit, crisp white shirt, and black tie.

"Why don't you love birds go dance while we do some more mingling?" Monica suggested with a sly grin.

"Mingling as in snooping?" Jackson drawled. Monica winked but didn't answer, just looped her arm with Jenna's and the two of them disappeared into the crowd.

"Shall we?" Jackson nodded toward the dance floor and I found myself being swung into his arms. I laughed. "Absolutely." Winding my arms around his neck I let my body sway with his, utterly content in this perfect moment.

"I'm sorry about your birthday," Jackson whispered in my ear.

"There's nothing to be sorry about. It wasn't your fault someone died. I'm just sorry both Del and Tiny died on their birthdays." A shiver ran up my spine, causing the hairs on the back of my neck to stand on end. "Do you think the amulets only work on the person's birthday?"

"We don't know enough about them." Jackson ran a hand up my back, warming the trail of ice that had made me shiver. "But I know someone who does."

"My parents." I'd thought of it when I was talking with Carson about mom and dad. I could ask them about the amulets and was kicking myself that I hadn't thought of it before. "I need to talk to them anyway," I leaned back in his arms so I could see his face. "I have news."

"Oh?" Our dancing slowed to a shuffle. His eyes moved over my face, studying every inch. "What's happened?" The warmth of his hand as it slid around my nape was comforting. My life had just been turned upside down and I still wasn't sure what to make of this evening's events.

"There was a coven meeting tonight. Annie announced she wanted to retire."

"Okay." Jackson nodded. "So, what does that

mean? Is your Gran taking over?" He paused, considering that notion. "Lord help us."

I smiled. "No, Gran isn't taking over. Me. Annie wants me to be the next head witch."

Several seconds ticked by while Jackson looked at me, trying, I guessed, to get a read on how I felt about it. Truth was, I wasn't sure.

"You don't want the job?" His head cocked to one side as he considered me thoughtfully.

I sighed. "I don't know. It was a surprise. Annie gave me a warning recently that I was at risk of being booted out of the coven. Now for her to turn around and say I'm going to be the next head witch? It makes my head spin."

"But you went to tonight's meeting. So, I assume you're in."

"And that's why you're a detective."

"What would happen if you said no? That you don't want the head witch position."

I gnawed on my lower lip. "I'm not sure. Maybe Annie chooses someone else? Or they have an election or something?"

"And when do you have to give her an answer?"

"That's just it. I didn't really get the option, Annie just announced it like it was a done deal. I'm not sure I can get out of it. But then, I'm not sure I want to either. The truth is, I don't know what I want." I pouted and Jackson chuckled, rubbing his thumb over my cheek.

"You'll make an awesome head witch."

"Yeah, she will!" Gran chortled, interrupting us. "Can I cut in?" She elbowed her way between us without waiting for an answer and I gracefully conceded. Handing my boyfriend over I whispered in Gran's ear, "no groping." Then headed off to find Jenna and Monica.

We'd just refreshed our glasses when it happened. A commotion in the ladies' bathroom. Gran was still on the dancefloor with Jackson, so I knew she wasn't behind whatever had happened. I assumed it was someone getting up to mischief, maybe releasing a water sprout as a practical joke, or spelling the mirrors to make your reflection an ugly old crone. What I didn't expect was to hear that Edith Russell was dead on the bathroom floor.

"What?" Jenna, Monica, and I all looked at each other in horror. "Monica? Can you go..." I didn't finish getting the words out, she was off, faster than the eye can see. The band had stopped playing and the town hall echoed with whispers of shock. Jackson approached, resting a hand on my shoulder. "I'll go see what's happened. Wait here."

I nodded, worry gnawing at my gut. I had a very bad feeling I knew what had happened to Edith Russell. Monica reappeared, a breeze ruffling my hair.

"Well?" We all asked. Monica shook her head, face grim. "It's Mrs. Russell all right."

"And? Do you know what happened?" Jenna asked. Monica looked at me. "You're not going to like it."

"She had an amulet, didn't she?" The dread in my stomach hardened into a lead ball.

"Yes."

EIGHTEEN

"**I** saw Edith Russell." The ghost of Whitney Sims told us as we sat gathered in The Dusty Attic the following morning.

I narrowed my eyes as I studied Whitney, hovering near the self-help section. "What do you mean, you saw her? Do you mean you saw her ghost?"

Whitney huffed and crossed her arms over her chest. "So, I may have ducked into the town hall last night to check out the dresses. I miss getting dressed up, now that I'm a ghost I'm stuck in the same outfit I died in, and I tell you, as much as I love this navy dress with matching pumps, a change would be nice."

"We didn't see you there." Gran studied her nails. "Damn. I think I've got a chip."

"You wouldn't have. Unless you looked up. I was

hanging in the rafters. Get a birds-eye view of everything up there."

"Whitney. Did you see Edith Russell's ghost? Did you see what happened to her?" I said.

"I saw her spirit, yes. She came wandering out of the ladies' room, dazed and confused. She kept asking folks what had happened but of course, no-one could see or hear her. By this point, they were reacting to the fact that there was a dead woman on the bathroom floor, so the room was all a flutter. Then a big white light appeared, so bright it was dazzling. And Edith walked right on into that light with a smile on her face." Whitney finished on a wistful note.

"You didn't want to go into the light? Hitch a lift into the next world?" I asked, surprised Whitney hadn't ridden Edith's coattails.

"Oh, believe me, I tried. I shot down there but by the time I got to it, the light had gone. Guess it wasn't my time." I couldn't tell if Whitney was upset that she'd missed the light or not. Whitney had one damn fine poker face, seems that had carried over into death.

"Did you see what happened in the bathroom?" Jenna asked. "Who gave Edith the amulet?"

"I didn't go to the ball to spy on women in the bathroom!" Whitney declared, spiraling up towards the ceiling.

"Hold up, Whitney." Jackson stood and crossed to

the murder board. "You may have seen something you don't realize is useful."

She immediately joined Jackson at the board, practically purring as she sidled up to him. "How can I help, Detective?"

Jenna snorted. "Death hasn't changed her. We ask for her help and she can't be bothered, but a man asks for help and she's all up in his business so fast you don't have time to blink."

"Hey!" Whitney pouted, tossing her blonde hair over her shoulder. "I resent that remark. Although..." she tapped a pink-tipped finger against her matching pink lips. "It's probably true."

Jackson cleared his throat. "Ladies please, can we stay on track?" He tapped the murder board, where he'd added Edith Russell. "As far as the police are concerned, Edith died from a massive heart attack. They say she was dead before she hit the floor. But we all know that's not the case. She died because her soul was reaped—thanks to whoever gave her the Astrudian Amulet."

"I can't see someone walking up to her in the bathroom and saying 'here, hold this will ya.'" I said.

"Agreed." He crossed his arms and waited.

"Her purse was on the floor next to her." Monica said. "The usual contents, a compact, lipstick, tissues."

"Whoever is using the amulets knows the victim

has to touch it. That's where they failed with you, Harper. You opened the box but you didn't take it out. We still don't know how Del received his amulet, but considering the way he died, it's clear he did touch it. It was in his pocket, only he could have put it there. And while there was an amulet on Tiny, her death doesn't match having her soul reaped. And the amulets the police had in evidence were stolen, telling us that whoever is behind this isn't done yet. Three amulets, three souls. Whatever deal they have going with the crossroads demon, they're not done yet."

"I'm betting whoever it is slipped it into Edith's purse. Then when she went to the bathroom to touch up her makeup she would have seen it, taken it out to look at it, wondering what it was and what it was doing in her purse." Monica said.

"Sounds plausible." Jackson nodded. "But there's something else between Del's case and Edith's."

"I know." I said. "The speed. Del's soul wasn't reaped immediately. We assume he received the coin, touched it, in the morning, then went out to work on the tractor. Do we have a timeline on that?" I asked, looking at Jackson.

"Not a precise one. An hour or two from when he had breakfast to when he died," Jackson said.

"Right. A couple of hours give or take. But with Edith? The amulet was in her hand. She'd touched it and the demon had taken her soul pretty much immediately."

"What does that mean though?" Monica asked.

"Probably means that time is running out. For whoever did the deal and was given the amulets. Maybe three amulets, three days?" Gran suggested. Jackson snapped his fingers and pointed at Gran. "I think you're right." He said. "Which means whoever is behind this is getting desperate. They probably only have a few hours left to target a third soul. And there's still one amulet in play."

"We can't exactly put the town in lockdown and tell everyone to stay home until tomorrow." Jenna piped up. She'd been busy on her laptop, writing up the story from last night's events I assumed. "And with the coroner ruling Mrs. Russell's death natural causes, you can't exactly announce we have a serial killer in our midst. As far as the public is aware, Tiny's is the only murder."

"Jenna's right," I said. "The only way to find that third amulet and take it out of play is to find Tiny's killer."

"Hate to play Devil's advocate, but..." Jenna interrupted, "you're assuming Tiny's killer is behind the amulets. That they planted an amulet on Tiny after she'd died as a way to, what? Trick the crossroads demon? You also have to consider that we just might be looking at two different perpetrators here. The person with the amulets may have planted one on Tiny after the killer had done their work. Maybe they discovered Tiny, thought she wasn't dead and they could take advantage of the situation, reap her soul anyway."

Jackson crossed his arms and thought about what Jenna had said. "That is plausible, I guess, but my gut is telling me that isn't the case."

"I vote we follow Jackson's gut," Gran announced.

Nodding in agreement we turned our attention to the murder board and the list of suspects and clues.

"Well, it can't be Glen Weaver." I pointed out. "He's still in custody. Wrongly accused of Tiny's murder."

"He'll be out on bail today," Jackson said. "But you're right. He's not behind this."

"Jessie Mathis?" Monica questioned. "Did he kill Tiny because she wouldn't sign to join his team?"

"Nope." Jackson declared. "His alibi checks out. He's been dealing with Tiny remotely, he didn't arrive in Whitefall Cove until yesterday afternoon in time for last night's fundraiser."

"Yeah, he told me he was in Florida at the time of her death, practicing at the Daytona International Speedway," I confirmed. "I also spoke with Jodie Bell last night. It was her car Tiny was working on when she died. Not only did Jodie have no motive, she didn't have the opportunity either. She's the event manager for the Singh Corporation and she was busy getting ready for the fundraiser. A ton of witnesses can place her at the town hall."

"Which leaves us, Roxanne Mann." Jackson tapped her name. "You're the only witness who can put her at Tiny's garage."

"Right." I nodded. "Funny thing. I talked with Jodie last night about inviting Tiny to the fundraiser and she said Tiny wasn't invited. Apparently they only issue invitations to VIP guests, and those VIPs are one's with deep pockets and big checkbooks. Of which Tiny was not."

"About Roxanne." Jenna glanced up from her laptop. "Harper told us about that last night, so I did some digging into Roxanne's background."

"Don't you ever sleep?" Monica asked. Jenna lifted one shoulder. "Not when we've got news stories like these happening in our idyllic little town."

"What did you find out?" Jackson asked.

"Something very interesting. I could only trace Roxanne's digital footprint back ten years. Before that? Nothing. No social media, no emails, no sign of her."

Jackson perked up. "Really? I'll look into that some more. She should have a driver's license and social security info, I'll see what I can dig up."

"We're really saying we think Roxanne Mann is behind this? That miss designer duds would get her hands dirty and bash Tiny's head in with a steel pole?" Monica began pacing, chewing on the inside of her cheek. "I'm not seeing it. A woman who spends hours at the beauty salon, who is polished within an inch of her life. Murder?"

"Desperate times call for desperate measures," I said. "I agree, killing Tiny that way seems so far out of character for Roxanne it's beyond a stretch. But we think Tiny was blackmailing her. So there's a motive. Opportunity? I guess so. I saw her in the garage that morning. She could have easily returned later in the day. We know she made a five thousand cash payment to Tiny. Maybe Tiny changed the terms—it's not like she hasn't done that before."

"What would Tiny have over Roxanne that she could blackmail her over?" Monica asked.

"It usually comes down to money or sex," Jackson answered. "And given what Jenna told us, that she can't find any information on Roxanne outside of ten years, that's definitely a string we can pull." Then he pinned me with a gaze. "Tell me about this blackmail theory."

I quickly filled him in on what Gran had overheard at the hair salon, and that it married up with what I'd found in Tiny's accounts. Local gossip had Roxanne withdrawing two separate lots of cash from the ATM. Five thousand a pop. Tiny's ledger had corresponding entries with no annotation on where the money had come from.

"Wait!" I gasped, a lightbulb going off in my brain. "Jenna." I pointed at my best friend. "You said you can't find anything on Roxanne Mann beyond ten years, right?"

She nodded. "Correct."

"And we know these amulets are currency for a crossroad demon, right?"

"Yep." Gran nodded.

"Don't you get it?" I swung around in a circle, looking at the puzzled faces of my nearest and dearest. "What if Roxanne Mann did a deal with a crossroads demon ten years ago, and now her time is up? Now he wants her soul. So he..." I paused, looked up at the ceiling as if the answers were written there. Of course they weren't, all I could see was the ghost of Whitney as she drifted around above us. "What if the demon gave her a new identity? A new life? A rich life! But now it's time to pay up, but of course, she wouldn't want to. Who would? So she's somehow managed to strike up another deal. More souls in exchange for hers? Maybe."

Jackson's phone buzzed. "Ward." He answered, his face a mask. I chewed my lip, please don't let it be another death, please don't let it be another death, I chanted silently.

"On my way." He hung up. My heart sank. There

was one missing amulet in play. My theory that it could only be used on someone's birthday was blown out of the water by Edith Russell's death last night. It had not been her birthday. And that changed everything. Now anyone was a potential victim.

"What's happened?" I asked, dying to know but not wanting to hear the answer.

"Relax. No-one's dead." He assured me, though the frown on his face told me that whatever had happened, it wasn't good. "Tiny's house has been firebombed."

"What?" We all said in unison, a cacophony of high-pitched squawks laced with incredulity.

Jackson held up a hand to shush us. "It's okay. The damage is minimal. Whoever threw the Molotov cocktail needs to practice their pitch, it barely reached the house."

"A drive-by?" Jenna asked, already on her feet and ready to cover the story.

"Looks like." Snatching up his jacket from where he'd tossed it on the back of the sofa when he'd arrived, he shot me a look. "Driz is fine."

I felt all sorts of awful. I'd forgotten about the demon currently in lockdown in Tiny's house.

Gran stiffened. "You don't think this was a hate crime do you?" She snapped, an underlying tone of steel in her voice. Gran didn't arc up about much, but when she did, watch out, she'd strip your skin from your hide with her sharp words.

Jackson shrugged. "Can't rule anything out at this stage. Did anyone else know Driz is here? Did you tell anyone?"

Gran sniffed and studied her fingernails. "No." Her voice was sullen and the way she was avoiding eye contact told me she was telling a big fat lie.

"Gran," I warned. "Who did you tell about Driz?"

"I didn't tell anyone about him." She objected.

"But?" I prompted, knowing there was more to this.

"Okay fine. I took Ace out for a walk—"

"You took a bird out for a walk?" I snorted. "How did that work? Did he fly away?"

"He did not fly away because he is basically naked. No feathers means minimal air time." She told me. "But a few people stopped and asked about him."

"Ahhhh." I put two and two together. Gran was out walking the ugliest bird in the world. People naturally gravitated towards Ace. Most likely because they weren't too sure exactly what the poor creature was. "And you told them he was Tiny's bird? And maybe that led into gossiping about Tiny and the secret demon lover she kept hidden in her house?"

Gran totally ignored me and turned to Jackson. "I'm coming with you. I want to check on Driz, make sure he's okay. Is the house habitable? If he can't stay there he can come stay with me."

"Wait. I'm coming too. It's going to be a bumper issue of the Whitefall Cove Tribune this week." Jenna followed Gran outside onto the sidewalk.

Jackson dropped a kiss on my lips. "I'll call you. Stay out of trouble." Then he joined them outside. I could see them arguing about whose car to take, eventually deciding Gran would go with Jackson and Jenna would take her own vehicle, since she needed to return to the Tribune offices later and submit the story.

"I guess that's a wrap for the murder club today." Monica drawled from her sprawled position in an armchair.

"Temporarily postponed." I looked at the stunningly gorgeous vampire who was also one of my best friends. "How do you feel about joining me later this evening, once the sun is down?"

A smirk curled her red lips. "Why, Harper Jones, I'm intrigued. You have a plan?"

I grinned back at her. "I do. And the fewer people who know about it the better."

"Do tell!" She hadn't moved from her elegant slouch if you could even call slouching elegant, but somehow Monica made it look elegant and sexy as hell with one leg swinging over the arm of the chair.

"I want to search Roxanne's house for the missing amulet."

Her smile was wide. "A little B&E? I'm in. I assume you don't want the others to know about this?"

"You assume right. Jackson—of course—would not approve. And Gran can't be trusted to keep her mouth shut. And while I know Jenna would be up for it, she's busy with the paper. I say you and I can do a little re-con."

"I am two hundred percent in." She stood, smoothing her hands down her leather-clad thighs. "Where shall we meet? And when?"

Carson Singh's house was a mansion. Monica and I stood at the gate and peered up the long driveway to the house looming out of the darkness. The gates were, of course, locked. It had conveniently left my mind that rich people would naturally guard all their possessions with locks and alarms.

"Two options," Monica said, glancing at me sideways. "I can break the lock. That'll get us through the gates no problem, but there may be an alarm. And if there isn't, well they're going to know someone busted through their gate, because while I can smash it, I sure can't fix it."

I adjusted the black hoodie covering my head. "What's the second option?"

"Uh, hello, big super-duper witch! You can rustle up some magic." It was perfectly obvious only, yet again, using my magic hadn't occurred to me. Was Annie out of her mind selecting me to replace her? When I didn't reply Monica turned to me and clasped my shoulders. "Come on, Jones." She cajoled. "Surely you can rustle up something? Levitate us over the gate maybe? Or unlock the gate with a magical skeleton key?"

"You're right." I said with false bravado. "I've got this." Holding out both hands I summonsed my magic. A bright blue ball appeared, small to begin with but as I moved my hands it grew and stretched until it was surrounding Monica and me.

"Ooooh. Pretty." Monica said, trailing a finger through the sparkling light. "But also, bright. Might want to get a move on before someone in the house notices a bright assed light out here."

Damn it, she was right. I hurried things along, quickly lifting us over the huge wrought iron gates and depositing us safely on the other side. Dusting my hands together I followed Monica as she darted up the driveway, keeping to the shadows. A gust of wind blew my hair across my face and I tightened the hood, tucking the strands beneath the fabric. Thunder rumbled overhead.

"Storms rolling in," Monica said, eyeing the sky. All I could see was black, the clouds obliterating the stars and moon. Perfect if you want to try your hand at a little break and enter, but also, spectacularly spooky at the same time. There was a chill in the air, reminding me that the seasons were changing and soon it would be winter. I tugged the zipper a little higher until it was snug up under my chin. "You're lucky you don't feel the cold." I grumbled.

Monica ignored me, studying the mansion before us. Lights shone out of some of the windows, the rest of the building was in darkness. "Are you sure they're not home?"

I frowned. "Jenna said they're meant to be at a private dinner party this evening."

"Maybe they left some lights on for when they get home."

"Could be." My nerves were starting to get the better of me. Breaking into Carson and Roxanne's home had seemed like a good idea, but now, standing outside the big, dark, spooky house, I wasn't so sure. And I knew in advance that Jackson would be pissed when he found out. If he found out. Come on Harper, big girl panties.

"Let's go round the back," I said, heading down the side of the house. "It'll be less exposed."

"You look jittery. You okay?"

I straightened my spine and squared my shoulders. "I'm fine. Let's do this."

"That's my girl. I'm going to do a quick reconnaissance around the outside, peek through a couple of windows to make sure they're not home after all."

"Good idea. I'll meet you at the back door." She was gone in the blink of an eye and I continued down the side of the house, my hands running along the stone wall to guide my way. Everything sounded super loud to my ears. The crunching of gravel beneath my runners, the harsh rasping of my breath, my heartbeat thundering through my veins. I spotted Monica as soon as I rounded the corner, leaning back against the brick wall near the rear entrance of the house, the light from an old fashioned lantern casting a yellow light over her.

"All clear." She told me as I approached. "You were right, they just left some lamps on."

"Right." I nodded, approached the back door, and used my magic to turn the snib. With a soft click, the door swung open. "Let's just hope there isn't an alarm." I whispered, more to myself than Monica, "because I'm not sure my magic could solve that one."

The back door opened into a wide passageway and there on the wall, an alarm pad. But it was dark, no lights flashed, nothing beeped.

"Curious." Monica tapped it. "Not armed. I wonder why they didn't set it?"

"Let's just search for the amulet and get out of here," I replied. My sense of heebie-jeebies intensified. The sooner we were out of this house, the better. "Remember, if you find the amulet, don't touch it."

"Honey, I'm not sure I have a soul for the crossroads demon to reap." And then she was gone, leaving me to contemplate if vampires have souls and would the amulet work on a vampire.

NINETEEN

Carson Singh's mansion was a maze of rooms and hallways and searching for the amulet was the proverbial needle in a haystack. Even with Monica helping it would take us hours to search the entire house, as it was, at least two hours had passed when Monica found me in the third story cloakroom, checking pockets of the coats hanging there. Why have a cloakroom on the third floor? Who knows? I assumed the coats hanging here were old, maybe out of fashion, rejects from Roxanne and Carson's own wardrobe.

"We've got trouble," Monica said, leaning a hand on either side of the door frame she peered in at me.

"Oh?" I glanced up from where I'd been patting down a full-length fur coat.

"They're home."

"What!" I heard it then. The slamming of car doors. "Shit," I whispered. "We need to get out of here."

"Roger that."

We bolted down the stairs to the second landing, then the first and had just begun the final descent to the ground floor when the door opened. I plastered myself against the wall and screwed my eyes shut, willing them not to look up. If they didn't look up, they wouldn't see us. After what felt like an eternity their footsteps receded and I sagged in relief.

"Know any invisibility spells?" Monica whispered in my ear. "I mean, I'm pretty sure I can get out of here undetected. You, on the other hand..."

"Actually..." I had been meaning to work on that very thing. Not rendering myself invisible per-se, but an invisibility bubble. I knew I could produce a force field that I could bend and stretch to accommodate a small group of people. If I could adapt that force field to render the people inside invisible? That would totally work. Hurrying back up the stairs to the first landing, I called forth my magic and spun a force field around myself.

"Can you see me?" I whispered to Monica.

"Yup." She was watching me from the top of the staircase.

I amped up my magic. "How about now?"

I felt a rush of wind as Monica appeared in front of

me. "Oh my God, you did it." She reached out a hand and poked me in the chest.

"Ow." I slapped her hand away. "I'm still here. It's just an illusion spell. Here, get inside." I grabbed her wrist and tugged her into the bubble with me. "Okay, move slowly. They can still hear us and, heaven forbid, touch us."

"This is so cool. It's just like Harry Potter and the invisibility cloak." Monica grinned, clasping my hand as we crept toward the staircase.

"I guess it is." I couldn't contain my own smile as we made our way back down to the ground floor. We were in the hallway and the back door was in sight when we heard Roxanne and Carson talking in the kitchen. Sneaking forward on tiptoes we peeked around the doorframe.

Carson handed Roxanne a glass, followed by two pills. "Take these, you'll feel better."

"Thanks, Honey." Roxanne tossed the pills into her mouth and took a sip of water to wash them down. "Sorry to cut the evening short." She rubbed two fingers at her temples and Carson immediately moved behind her to massage her shoulders.

"It's been a busy few days," he said. "You're exhausted. I'm not surprised you have a headache. Why not have an early night?"

"You know, I think I will." Her smile was tight as

she turned, reached up on tiptoes, and kissed his cheek.

We quickly ducked back out into the hallway as she approached, flattening ourselves against the wall and holding our breath as she drew level with us. She paused, then turned her head, looking directly at us. My lungs were screaming for air but I daren't breathe for fear she'd hear me. Nothing but my eyeballs moved as I risked a glance at Monica. Okay for her, she didn't need to breathe air, but she did a pretty awesome statue imitation, standing completely frozen.

Outside the storm intensified, a loud crack of thunder shook the windows. Carson stuck his head around the doorframe. "Everything okay?"

"Hmmm?" Roxanne shook her head, then continued on towards the staircase, "Everything's fine. Sorry, I just got one of those weird feelings you get—you know, like you're being watched."

Carson laughed. "Must be the ghosts messing with you again."

"Must be." Roxanne disappeared upstairs and Carson back into the kitchen. We were alone.

"We should follow her," I whispered to Monica. "If she is behind the amulets and the crossroads demon deal, time is running out for her."

"You think her going to bed early is a ruse?" Monica whispered back.

"Only one way to know for sure." Off we went,

hand in hand, creeping back up the staircase. Thankfully the master suite was on the first floor. Roxanne had left the door ajar and I peered inside. I couldn't see her, but I could hear a rustling sound, figured she was getting changed. Then she crossed my line of vision, dressed in plum silk pajamas. Flipping the covers back on the massive California king, she slid into bed. So much for that theory, seems like Roxanne really was going to bed.

Monica jerked her head, indicating we should leave. I nodded in agreement. I had no desire to hang around and watch someone sleep. For what felt like the millionth time that evening we returned downstairs and made it to the back door, slipping outside undetected. Once we'd cleared the gate at the bottom of the driveway, I dropped the spell and the magic bubble disappeared.

"Well?" Monica asked as we climbed into my car.

I shook my head, started the engine and reversed out from the overgrown track where I'd hidden the car from view of the main road. "I'm sure she's involved in this somehow. I just need to prove it."

Big, fat, raindrops splattered across the windscreen. Slow at first but picking up speed. "I've got a really bad feeling," I muttered under my breath.

"You sure it's not just the storm messing with you? All that atmospheric pressure? It's certainly adding a certain vibe to our evening activities."

Monica replied, a rumble of thunder punctuating her words.

I glanced at her out of the corner of my eye. "Maybe." I conceded with a sigh. My phone vibrated from my back pocket and I wriggled in my seat to retrieve it, tossing it to Monica. "Get that will you?"

Monica caught it and looked at the screen. "Hey, Jenna. Harper's driving. Lemme put you on speaker." After punching the speaker icon on the phone she held it up between us. "You're good to go."

"Where are you guys?" Jenna demanded. "We have news." I could hear Gran in the background, chattering away, most likely with Ace. Or Driz, who was temporarily in Gran's custody.

"We were doing a little recon," I explained. "We're on our way now. Are you...eating?" I could hear the distinct sound of chewing.

"You could have warned me that Driz is an exceptional cook," Jenna whined. "I've put on ten pounds since walking in the front door."

I laughed. "What did he make?"

She snorted. "What didn't he make you mean. There are pies, cakes, puddings. I hope you're hungry!"

"We'll be there in five," I promised. "So what did you find out."

"Nuh-uh. I'll tell you when you get here."

"Spoilsport." Monica disconnected the call and

dropped my phone into the cup holder. "Well, at least she had some success I suppose."

"Agreed." For our search of the Singh mansion had turned up nothing. Not that we'd had time to search it all, but still, we'd done the important parts. The main living areas, kitchen, bedroom. Although if you were hiding a dangerous amulet from your significant other, maybe you'd hide it someplace obscure. But time was running out and you'd need it close at hand. One more amulet. One more soul to reap. Maybe Roxanne had it in her evening purse. I was sorely tempted to turn around and drive back to double-check, but we were two minutes from Gran's and my stomach rumbled at the thought of pie. I wondered if it was cherry like Driz had made me before.

I needn't have worried about what type of pie it was for Jenna had been right. Gran's kitchen was stacked high with almost every bakery item you could possibly think of. Not only pies, cakes, and puddings, but doughnuts, buns, croissants, and sweet bread.

"Wow, Driz, you've outdone yourself." Hands on hips I surveyed the kitchen. Driz smiled, the overhead light catching his blue scales and making them sparkle.

"Thank you, Harper. What can I get you? Pie? I know you like my cherry pie."

"I do indeed." I nodded. He cocked his head, considered me for a moment before snapping his fingers. "I know. Try my new blend, appleberries, and cherryrocks pie."

"Errr..." I glanced at Gran, wondering if she was teaching Driz wrong words.

Gran snorted and lifted her nose in the air. "So I magic upped a couple of new species of berries, no big deal, and not against any laws." As an aside to Driz she stage whispered, "Harper can be a bit of a stickler for the rules."

"Son of a beach!" Screeched Ace from his cage in the corner.

"Gran!" I scolded. "What are you teaching that bird?"

"Well, it's better than 'don't touch that' a million times a day," Gran grumbled. "Now come, let's go sit and Jenna can finally spill the beans on her piece of news. I swear that girl is going to pee her pants or explode if she doesn't tell us soon."

Jenna and Monica were already in the living room, Jenna with three empty plates in front of her, Monica with a shot glass of...I peered closer. Could be tequila, could be vodka.

"Good, good, good." Jenna jumped up and waved me into her seat. "We're all here. Jackson is busy with the arson thing at Tiny's house, so we're starting without him—Harper you can bring him up to speed later."

"Fine." I took a bite of my appleberry and

cherryrock pie and almost died on the spot. It was the most delicious concoction I'd ever tasted. The sweetness of the apple and cherry combined with the tartness of the berries was perfection. My eyes rolled into the back of my head in orgasmic delight. "Driz!" I tapped my spoon on the side of my plate. "This is amazing! I don't know how you do it."

"Thank you, Harper."

"You should tell her your news." Gran nudged him with her elbow.

"Oh?" I looked from one to the other, wondering what plan Gran had hatched and that Driz, with little experience of Gran's coercing ways, had fallen in with.

"Driz is going to buy The Tea Leaf!" Gran jumped in before Driz even got his mouth open. "He'll have money from Tiny's estate and this will give him not only a job but ongoing income. And boy, can this demon cook. He's going to be a hit." The Tea Leaf was a café that had been boarded up when the two sisters running it had been arrested and sent to jail for murder.

"Actually...not a bad idea." For once Gran had a half-decent suggestion.

"Ahem." Jenna cleared her throat, reached out to place a hand on Driz's arm. "Not that your news isn't exciting. It is. And congratulations, I think you'll do wonderfully. But we have a murder investigation to get back to."

Driz inclined his head. "Of course. Please proceed."

"Come on then, I can see you're dying to tell us what you discovered. Spill."

"Well." Jenna heaved in a breath. "After Tiny's place was firebombed, Driz discovered Tiny had hidden this old beat-up biscuit tin under the front porch."

I blinked in surprise. A hiding place outside? Quite genius actually. For I'd searched her house and her garage, but not outside her house and definitely not under her porch. "What was in it?" I asked.

Jenna held up an old, faded, photograph. I peered at it. It was of a young woman. The photo was creased and slightly blurry. "Who's that?" Monica asked, reaching for it.

"None of us recognized her. So I took it into work and scanned it and ran it through a database."

"And?"

"That is Roxanne Mann."

We all gasped. I snatched the photo from Monica and studied it. I could see a slight resemblance, but the girl in the picture had to be eighteen or nineteen years old, and certainly wasn't the well-manicured and groomed Roxanne we knew of today.

"But there's more." Jenna was practically hopping from foot to foot. "Her name wasn't Roxanne Mann back then. Her name was Cole Ramirez."

"She was a he?" It took a lot to shock Gran but she

was definitely shocked now. She picked up Monica's drink and downed it in one gulp. But Jenna was shaking her head, "No, Cole can be a female name too."

"Not very common though," Monica said, rescuing her glass from Gran and getting up to pour herself another drink.

"Exactly. Not very common. So when you have an uncommon name—for a girl—and a criminal record, what do you do?"

"You change your name." I breathed. "She has a criminal record? What did she do?"

"Cole Ramirez killed a man when she was eighteen. Claimed it was self-defense. Spent two years in jail for manslaughter. Her family turned their back on her, so when she got out, she was on her own."

I waved the photo. "This is why Tiny was blackmailing her. Tiny knew who she was in her old life."

Jenna was nodding. "That's exactly what I thought. So I went back and tried to trace where their paths would have crossed—and how Tiny could have identified her. There was a race meet in Redmeadows, and Tiny was on the circuit back then. Roxanne's, or should I say Cole's, family was quite well off and they had shares in one of the other teams. So they were at the race meet that day."

"And then Roxanne moved to Whitefall Cove and Tiny recognized her?" Gran surmised.

"I assume that's what happened. Or something along those lines. I also think Roxanne's transformation from Cole to Roxanne was thanks to a crossroads demon. She came out of jail broke, disowned by her family, a bleak future in front of her. Yet look at her now, engaged to a millionaire, dressed in designer clothes, a corporate career."

"Except she traded her soul for that lifestyle. Or a new identity. And like we've said before, we assume that it's time for Roxanne to pay up." I pointed out. "The crossroads demon has pretty non-negotiable terms."

"Where were you two tonight anyway?" Jenna asked, eyes darting between Monica and me. Monica waved her hand at me, indicating I could have the pleasure of answering.

"We searched the Singh mansion." I admitted.

"That's my girl." Gran grinned, while Jenna blinked in shock. "Harper Jones, you broke in?"

"We said earlier desperate times call for desperate measures. I want to get that amulet before Roxanne uses it again and someone else loses a soul."

"And? Did you find it." She answered her own question. "Of course you didn't. You would have told us already if that were the case."

"She must have it with her, on her," I explained.

"We searched as much as we could before they came home."

"You got caught?"

"Almost," I told them what Monica and I had witnessed, that Roxanne had gone to bed early with a headache.

"This isn't making sense." Gran huffed. "If you're about to lose your soul to a decade-old deal, but you have the means to change the deal, to basically stay alive, why wouldn't you have used that amulet yet? I'd be tossing them around like frisbees. Here, catch!" She imitated throwing a frisbee through the air at Monica. "When someone throws something at you, you catch it, right?"

"True." Monica drawled. "But that isn't very subtle. Someone sure as hell would notice you doing that and if the people who caught your frisbee dropped down dead? Say hello to the pokey."

"Exactly!" I leaned forward to put my empty plate on the coffee table. "This is still murder. Roxanne has already spent two years in jail, there's no way she'd be careless with this. She has to make sure she's not caught. She planned this very carefully. Targeted her three victims. How fortuitous that we all shared the same birthday. What a perfect way to get the amulets into our hands—present them as gifts."

"Only that backfired." Jenna said. "You didn't touch yours. You left it in the gift box it came in."

"Only because I was in a hurry. Plus I've seen tons of artifacts, I thought it was something mom and dad had sent me for my birthday, I would have taken it out later."

"And Tiny? She couldn't have touched hers either, because she didn't die from having her soul reaped." Gran said.

"The killer—Roxanne—must have taken the gift box with her after she killed Tiny. There were no traces of a gift box." I chewed my lip, deep in thought. "Her carefully thought out plan backfired. Out of her three victims, only one actually touched the amulet. Mine was taken out of play by Annie. Which left Tiny. Roxanne must have called in that morning to see if the amulet had done its job. Maybe she tried to get Tiny to touch it and when that failed she lost her temper, took matters into her own hands."

"But she saw you that morning too. So she must have known you hadn't touched your amulet either. Why not attack you?" Jenna asked.

"Because I wasn't blackmailing her. If you were told you had to choose three people to die so that you could live, who would you choose? Your first choice would be the person blackmailing you, the person who knew your secret, the person you were paying a lot of money to stay quiet. Other than that, you probably wouldn't care who the others were. Me and Del were just convenient because of our birthdays."

"That makes sense when she targeted Edith Russell then. An older woman. Not a lot of questions would be asked, like she's old, hardly surprising she dropped down dead." Monica said.

Gran sniffed. "She wasn't that old. In her sixties."

"You know what I mean though." Monica argued. "She got a stroke of luck with Del because he died while driving his tractor. It crashed and rolled on him, so it looked like that was what killed him. An accident. But if Harper here suddenly dropped down dead? Questions would be asked. She's young and healthy. I think Roxanne had to re-think her strategy, especially when she lost her cool and killed Tiny."

"Her new strategy is what? Targeting the elderly?" Jenna asked.

"Oh my God." I breathed. "You're right. Desperate times call for desperate measures. We keep saying that. Come on, we have to go!" I jumped to my feet, heading for the door.

"What? Where? What's going on?" Gran asked, hurrying behind me. I turned to her. "Gran, you stay here with Driz and Archie. Keep them safe, okay?"

Gran reared back. "What? You think they're in danger?"

I shook my head. "No. I don't. But I need to know you guys are here, together. I think I know who Roxanne's third victim will be. I just hope I'm not too late. And if I'm wrong? I'm worried she may target you, to get back at me."

"We will stay here and be safe," Driz told me, resting a giant blue hand on Gran's shoulder. Monica and Jenna squeezed past him and joined me at the front door. "Where are we going?" Jenna asked.

"Shady Pines." I flung open the door and stepped outside, ignoring the rain. "I think she's going after Carson's grandmother, Ruth Singh."

TWENTY

"You really think Roxanne would murder her fiancée's grandmother?" Jenna asked, gripping the door handle as I screeched around a corner, my headlights cutting through the torrential downpour currently hammering Whitefall Cove.

"I don't think it was her initial plan," I said through gritted teeth as I gripped the steering wheel in a death grip. "More of a last-ditch attempt to save her own hide and it wouldn't hurt to inherit Ruth's fortune either."

"But we just saw her going to bed." Monica said from the back seat.

"I think that's to throw Carson off the scent. Go to bed early with a headache. Sneak out. Slip his grandmother the amulet, then sneak back into bed with Carson none the wiser." And with Ruth Singh being in her nineties, no-one would suspect foul play if she didn't wake up in the morning.

The parking lot of Shady Pines was deserted except for one other vehicle. A black BMW. My heart skipped a beat. Seems Roxanne was already here. *Were we too late?* Clambering out of my car we hurried inside, skidding to a halt at the reception desk where a middle-aged woman with bags under her eyes and headphones on, sat staring blankly at her computer, seemingly oblivious to our presence.

Monica slammed her hand down on the bell repeatedly.

"Okay, okay." The woman grumbled, tugging the headphones down around her neck. "Visiting hours are over. Come back tomorrow."

"This is an emergency." Elbows on the counter I leaned in, read the name badge pinned to her navy cardigan. "Helen, we need to see Mrs. Singh."

Helen glared at me, stood, and tapped at the notice taped to the counter. "Visiting hours are between ten and four daily. It is now—" she turned around and eyeballed the clock mounted on the wall behind her. "Eight forty-five. PM. Come. Back. Tomorrow."

"Why is reception open then?" Jenna demanded.

"For the residents. And those doors," she nodded at the double glass doors we'd just passed through.

"Get locked at nine. I suggest you get yourself on the other side of them before I call the police."

I glanced at Jenna, then Monica. Coming back tomorrow was not an option. I looked beyond Helen, to the large map of shady pines, just beneath the clock. Two large residential wings. East and West. At the rear of the property, independent living units, at least thirty of them. No time to search them all. And given Mrs. Singh's advanced age I doubted she was in an independent living unit. Which meant she was either in the East wing or West.

"Sorry to bother you." I smiled sweetly, and turned away, gesturing for Jenna and Monica to follow me. We gathered a few feet away. "Monica, can you search the East wing for Mrs. Singh? Jenna and I will go West." I touched Jenna's wrist. "Are you up for this? We're going to have to run."

"Of course!"

"Ready?" I whispered. They nodded. "Go!" We ran. Full sprint past the reception desk and down the corridor marked West wing. Monica was nothing but a blur as she headed toward the East wing.

"Hey!" Helen shouted. "Get back here." Her chair squeaked in protest as she propelled it back so fast it hit the wall. "That's it. I'm calling the cops. And security!" She screeched after us.

Sprinting down the corridor I scanned the names on the doors we passed. I could hear the blare of televisions from behind some, but others were quiet with no light peeking out from beneath the door. The West wing, it turns out, was more than one wing, it branched off into another three mini wings. We stopped, struggling to catch our breath as we eyeballed the sign for each area.

"Suites sounds like a goer." Jenna puffed. I nodded in agreement. Ruth Singh was loaded, no doubt she had a suite as opposed to a single room. "Let's go."

My hunch paid off. Even the carpet in the corridor was lusher, more opulent than the rest of the facility. Potted plants and large floral displays were artfully placed along the hallway, paintings with overhead lighting decorated the walls. And there, the third of the way down was a plaque with Ruth Singh's name engraved on it. Stopping outside the double doors I pressed my ear against the wood to listen. I could hear the soft murmur of voices but couldn't tell if it was someone talking or just the television.

Glancing at Jenna I wrapped my fingers around the handle and slowly turned. The door swung open on silent hinges and we crept inside. The suite was huge! More like a five-star apartment. We entered into a foyer with what appeared to be marble tiles on the floor. To my right was a kitchenette, my left a storage closet, straight ahead a huge open plan living and dining area. The back wall was made entirely of glass and overlooked what I assumed to be a garden, although with the storm raging outside and the rain lashing down, it was impossible to see clearly. Opposite the living room were two doors, both open. I could just make out a bedroom and bathroom, both massive in proportions.

Pressing my back against the kitchenette wall I eased forward, Jenna right behind me. The murmur of voices was louder now but I still couldn't make out the words. And...was that a man's voice? I risked a peek around the corner, blinked in shock, and quickly ducked out of view.

"Who is it?" Jenna mouthed.

"Carson Singh." I mouthed back.

"Who?" She mouthed. I rolled my eyes, moved back so she could take my place and look around the corner for herself. Her mouth formed a perfect O when she turned back to face me.

"Ladies, you may as well come out, I know you're there." Carson called, startling us both.

"Busted," Jenna whispered.

"Hi. Sorry!" I blurted, stepping into view, my eyes darting from Carson where he was reclining in an armchair looking incredibly relaxed and oh so debonair, to Ruth Singh, who was in a wheelchair, a throw rug over her lap, her eyes narrowing as she looked me up and down.

"Why are you here?" Carson asked, crossing his legs, one ankle resting on the opposite knee, pointing the remote at the television, and hitting mute. That explained the murmur of voices.

"We were looking for Roxanne," I explained.

"Who?" Ruth Singh shouted. Carson rolled his eyes, then leaned forward and shouted back, "they're looking for Roxanne."

"She's not here." Mrs. Singh yelled.

"I can see that," I muttered.

"Sorry about the shouting," Carson said. "She doesn't like putting her hearing aids in. You're looking for Roxanne? What makes you think she's here?"

I shrugged helplessly. "Saw her car out front."

"Ahh." He nodded. "We both drive black BMWs. Easy to get them confused I suppose. Anyway, Roxanne is home in bed, having an early night." He looked from me to Jenna and back again. "Anything I can help you with?"

I didn't know what to make of this turn of events. I'd been so sure Roxanne was here, about to hand Mrs. Singh an amulet but to find her sitting comfortably, visiting with her grandson? I was, quite bluntly, gobsmacked.

"Mrs. Singh?" I moved closer to the elderly woman. "Has Roxanne given you a gift lately? One that looks like a very old coin?"

Just as Mrs. Singh said, "what's that dear?" and cupped a hand to her ear, Carson said at the same time, "you mean one like this?"

My eyes rounded at the Astrudian amulet he held up.

"You!" Jenna squeaked in surprise. I motioned for her to come closer, for while my attention had been on the amulet, I now noticed he held a gun in the other hand. One aimed directly at us. I blinked slowly and called forth my protective bubble, stretching it over myself, Jenna, and Mrs. Singh.

"You made a deal with the crossroads demon," I said. "But why? It can't be for money, your family has plenty. Unless you don't? Unless you ran the family business into the ground?"

Carson smiled a sad, wistful smile. "You're right. It's not about money."

"If not money, then what?"

"Love."

"Love?" My voice betrayed my surprise. "You have Roxanne, don't you love her?" I was so confused.

"Exactly. I have Roxanne, and yes, I do love her. Too much I fear."

"I'm really not following," I admitted.

"You coming here tonight has been fortuitous. Rather than one soul, I can deliver two. And spare Grandmother at the same time."

"What's that?" Yelled Mrs. Singh. "Why are you pointing the remote at these women, Carson?"

He chuckled softly, then jerked the gun at Jenna and I. "Over there, both of you, now!" Reluctantly I moved away from Mrs. Singh and shuffled toward the windows where he was pointing. I felt my bubble stretch, and stretch, and stretch, until it snapped, leaving Jenna and I protected but Mrs. Singh vulnerable. I wondered if Carson knew that, knew I had this ability, knew that separating us meant I had to choose one or the other.

He moved to stand behind his Grandmother but kept the gun trained on us, the amulet in his other hand. I swallowed. All he had to do was hand the amulet to his grandmother and she'd be dead and there was nothing I could do to stop him.

"Wait!" I pleaded. "You don't have to do this, Carson. She's your grandmother."

He laughed. "Oh, don't be foolish. Now that you're here I can spare her. Don't worry, she's safe. You'd do better worrying about yourself. And your pretty friend."

I glanced at Jenna who was eyeballing Carson with a ferocious glare. I caught sight of a flash of red and glanced down to where she was gripping her phone in her fist. She was recording. Smart girl.

"Can you just tell us why?" I asked.

"A dying wish?" He jeered.

"If you like."

He considered me for several long silent seconds. I should have been worried, but I wasn't. I knew Jenna and I were safe in my bubble. It would protect us from the amulet and any bullets. My biggest concern was when he realized he couldn't use us, that he couldn't have our souls, he'd take his grandmothers. I tilted my head, considering the logistics. He'd have to approach us, get close enough to force the amulet onto our skin. Which meant once he realized he couldn't, he'd have to cross the room to get back to his grandmother. A scant few seconds, but it would be long enough for me to transfer the bubble from me and Jenna and back to Mrs. Singh. Risky as hell, but doable. In the meantime if I could keep him talking, and Helen the receptionist had followed through on her threat of calling security and the police, we just might all get out of this alive.

He heaved a sigh. "Sure. Why not." He began to pace, back and forth behind his grandmother. I was grateful she couldn't hear any of this, didn't realize her grandson held us at gunpoint.

"Roxanne is in trouble." I heard it then, the world of pain in his words. "I knew when I first laid eyes on her three years ago she was the one. The one girl I actually wanted to marry. Oh there had been plenty of women before her, and they were fun, some were with me for my money, some weren't. But I didn't love any of them. Until Roxanne."

"Oh, but she played it cool. Made me work for it." He chuckled. "Turned down my first two proposals because she didn't want me to think she was marrying me for my money. Which was funny because she has her own fortune."

"But eventually she said yes. You're engaged." I pointed out. "Or is that all thanks to the crossroads demon?"

"Nope, it was all down to me. Guess I just wore her down."

"Where does the crossroads demon come in then? It wasn't a straight-out deal, your soul for your deepest desire. No. He gave you currency, Astrudian amulets, three coins in exchange for...what? What was worth so much it would take three souls to pay for it?"

"Roxanne's soul."

I blinked. He'd traded three souls for Roxanne's? "Wait. You're saying...Roxanne already had a deal in place with the crossroads demon?"

He nodded, face grim. "She was young and in a tight spot, couldn't see a way out. So she made a deal. Only it's almost time to pay up." I remembered what Jenna had found out, that Roxanne had changed her name after being in jail for manslaughter.

"And she told you all this?" Jenna asked.

"Things came to a head recently." He nodded.

"What things?"

"Tiny's blackmail for one."

"You know about that?"

"I didn't. Not initially. But I could see Roxanne was upset. Really upset. And she finally broke down and told me everything. The manslaughter charge, the jail term, the deal with the crossroads demon for a new life."

"And you were okay with that?"

He shrugged. "You gotta do what you gotta do. I'm a businessman. I get it. But Tiny was becoming a problem. Initially Roxanne wasn't bothered with paying her off. Five grand here or there was nothing. But as the date of the wedding approached, Tiny got greedy. Said once we were married it would be fifty thousand a pop."

"That's a lot of money."

"It is. And not one you can hide in an accounting error. Or write off as a couple of pairs of shoes. But she had bigger problems than Tiny. Her deal with the crossroads demon was due before we'd have chance to walk down the aisle."

"So…what happened next? You thought you could re-negotiate the deal?"

"I knew Roxanne couldn't. Once a deal is struck the terms are concrete. I researched it, thoroughly, found the Astrudian amulets, and offered my own deal. I exchanged Roxanne's soul for three others."

"And obviously the crossroads demon agreed because here we are," Jenna said.

"It's a done deal. I have one more soul to go." He glanced at his watch. "With three hours to spare."

"And if you fail to deliver three souls? What?

Obviously Roxanne's deal still stands. So she's gone. But if you fail, is it your soul on the line?"

He inclined his head. "Precisely. But I won't fail." He took a step forward.

"Hold on." I held out a hand to stop him. "What happened with Tiny then? Why kill her? Why not take her soul? I see that you tried."

He raised his eyes to the ceiling and blew out an exasperated breath. "We had it planned perfectly. Three birthdays. Three amulets. We left them as gifts for each of you. Del opened his immediately and lifted the amulet out. Boom. One soul down. Then you, Harper. You opened the gift box but apparently didn't touch it. But that's okay, we still had time, we assumed you'd eventually lift the amulet out of the box to get a closer look at it, maybe show your parents. Either way, you'd touch it. But Tiny? Roxanne swung by the garage to make sure Tiny had the amulet. She saw the box, unopened, in the trash."

"That's what she was doing there that morning?"

He nodded. "She was furious. And of course, as soon as Tiny saw her she extorted more money out of her."

"So she killed her," Jenna said.

"Nope. I did." Carson admitted. "I slipped Roxanne a sleeping pill, waited until she was out, then went down to the garage myself."

Jenna's breath hitched. "You didn't go to talk to

Tiny! You went with the express intent of murdering her." I could practically see the lightbulb go off above her head.

"I'd hoped to make it look like an accident. Didn't care if it didn't. Only I misjudged the blow to her head. Seems I'd killed her outright when my intention was to mortally wound her, give the amulet enough time to do its job." He shrugged. "I failed on the soul collection but my objective was always to see Tiny dead, so it's still a win in my book." He glanced at his watch. "And there you have it, ladies. The full story. And now, if you don't mind, I have a soul to reap. Two, in fact, I'm sure the crossroads demon won't mind if I use the amulet twice."

I'd been so engrossed in his version of events that his approach took me by surprise. One second he was behind his grandmother the next he was in front of us and thrusting the amulet at me, trying to press it against my chest. Only, of course, my bubble kept a protective layer between me and the amulet.

"What the hell?" He frowned, looked down at the amulet, then back at me. He tried again.

"Is it meant to work straight away?" I asked innocently.

"The closer we get to midnight, the faster it works, so yes. You should be dead. Why aren't you?" He looked me up and down. "Of course. I forgot. You're a witch." He began pacing. "Which means you've probably got some sort of protection spell in place. Smart. Very smart." He approached again and pressed the amulet against Jenna. "Figured you'd extended it to your friend, but worth a try."

He tapped the gun against his thigh, then lifted his arm and aimed it at his grandmother. Jenna and I gasped.

"How about this." He ground out. "You drop that spell or I shoot her."

I looked at Mrs. Singh, horrified to think what was going through the poor woman's mind, seeing her grandson pointing a gun at her. I needn't have worried, she was asleep, her chin resting on her chest, a light snore reaching our ears. But now I was in a quandary. I couldn't split my bubble in two. I could protect Jenna and myself, or Mrs. Singh. In the end, it wasn't a hard decision to make.

"Don't shoot." I stepped forward, out of the bubble, but kept it in place around Jenna. "But you don't get both of us," I warned. He eyeballed me, then nodded.

"Fair enough." He stepped closer, held the amulet up in his left hand, and taunted, "one small flaw in your plan, Harper Jones. I take your soul and you're dead and your magic dies with you."

Crap! He was right. I'd thought I could protect Jenna, but I'd failed. The amulet was so close to my skin

I could feel its pull, knew I had nanoseconds to act, tried to get my head around the fact that I'd monumentally stuffed up and Jackson was going to be so pissed at this turn of events when suddenly the amulet was gone and Carson was left standing in front of me holding nothing.

"I don't think so, buddy." Monica jeered, standing between Mrs. Singh and her grandson.

This time I didn't hesitate. I snapped out a blast of magic that catapulted Carson into the ceiling. His head hit with a painful crunch before I slammed him back into the floor. The gun skidded across the floor and Jenna ran for it, snatching it up and aiming it at the man groaning on the carpet. Flakes of plaster fluttered down from the ceiling.

"Perfect timing," I said to Monica, holding a hand to my chest to catch my breath. That had been a close call. Too close for comfort.

"How are you able to hold that?" Jenna asked, nodding at the amulet in Monica's hand.

"This?" She waved it around. "I'm a vampire. I'm already dead. Therefore no soul. No living soul anyway." She cocked her head. "Now what? We call the cops?"

"The receptionist has probably alerted them to the fact that we're here." I said. "But I have a better idea. Can you carry him?"

"Sure." Monica slid the amulet into the back

pocket of her jeans and then hauled Carson over her shoulder in a fireman's hold.

"What's the plan?" Jenna asked.

"Monica, take Carson's car and drive him home. We'll meet you there. We're going to make it look like we were never here, which means magicking up some repairs to the ceiling, and getting out of here without being seen."

Jenna snorted. "How do you expect to do that?"

"Oh, you're going to like this." Monica chuckled, heading towards the door. "I'll meet you at the Singh mansion. What about Roxanne?"

"I'm pretty sure he drugged her, slipped her a couple of sleeping pills instead of headache pills. I bet she's still sound asleep in bed."

"I'll see you there." And she was gone in a puff of wind.

TWENTY-ONE

"Okay, who wants pie?"

Driz approached carrying a tray containing two pies and four cups of coffee. He wore a huge smile and a dainty, frilly, floral apron over his bedazzled denim overalls.

"Congratulations." I smiled, clearing the condiments aside to make room for the tray. "The Tea Leaf looks amazing."

Driz had been granted permanent residency status and had used Tiny's savings to purchase The Tea Leaf. Today was the grand re-opening day.

"I have all of you to thank." Driz replied. "Without your support, I'm not sure the citizens of Whitefall Cove would have welcomed me as warmly as they have."

"Are you nuts?" Gran sniffed. "Your baked goods are to die for."

"People keep saying that but I'm not so sure that is the correct slogan for my marketing." He frowned, then slid an oversized hand into the tiny pocket of his apron, tearing the stitching as he retrieved a well-worn photograph. I waved a little magic his way to repair the damage and patted his arm. "Tiny would be proud."

"She would, wouldn't she?" He sighed wistfully, a melancholy expression flitting across his face before he was all smiles once more. "Please. Enjoy. These are...what is the saying? On the roof?"

"On the house." Jackson chuckled.

"Yes. On the house. No payment required." His head swiveled, his ears picking up a sound none of us heard. "That is the timer in the kitchen," he said, "I must retrieve the buns."

We watched as the giant blue demon wove his way through the tables, stopping and smiling and saying hello to his patrons along the way.

"He's settled in well," Jackson commented, sliding a serve of pie onto a plate and handing it to me, before doing the same for Gran and Jenna. I passed around the coffees.

"Great article on the Singh's, Jenna." Jackson drawled, spooning sugar into his coffee and stirring.

She winked, "thanks," and shoved a spoonful of pie into her mouth.

Carson Singh and Roxanne Mann had been found deceased in their bed, victims of a gas leak. Jenna had written a revealing expose on Roxanne Mann and her previous life and identity, along with exposing Carson as Tiny's murderer. Although the police had no evidence to substantiate her claims, she had the recording of his confession, but it didn't amount to much when both parties were already dead, their souls claimed by the crossroads demon.

"So." Gran glanced around surreptitiously, then slipped a hip flask out of her purse and added a dash of goodness knows what into her coffee. "I think we should have a belated birthday party for Harper."

"What?" I choked. "No! No way. I didn't want a party when it was my birthday and I certainly don't want one now."

Jenna grinned, then scooped up another mouthful of pie. Just before she shoved it in her mouth she said, "I think that's a great idea."

"Traitor." I grumbled, "I can't. I have too much going on."

Gran laughed, a loud foghorn burst of sound. "Rubbish. Don't be hiding behind your new coven duties, I've been second-in-charge longer than you've been alive, I know exactly how the coven runs and how much work it requires. It is not a twenty-four-seven job."

I had a sinking feeling I was going to be outvoted on this. I'd fought hard the first time around not to have a party, just a low key evening with my beloved who, come to think of it, was now looking at me with a certain look on his face. I narrowed my eyes and studied him, saw the blush of color hit his cheekbones and his eyes slide away.

"Noooooo." I pointed a finger at him. "Not you too. How could you betray me this way?"

His dimple flashed. "Sorry, babe, but I happen to agree with your Gran on this one. It's been a hell of a year. Everyone wants to blow off some steam. A birthday party seems like a pretty good opportunity."

"You're right. It has been a big year, and I get that maybe y'all want to kick back and have fun—not that Gran needs an excuse to do that." I added. "But I don't need or want a birthday party. Seriously. I don't want a party to be about me. But I'm not opposed to putting on some sort of celebration."

"If not you, then who?" Gran slugged back the rest of her coffee, then topped up the empty cup with whatever was in her flask.

"How about something for Driz? A welcome to Whitefall Cove type thing? And a bit of a memorial for Tiny." I suggested.

"You know that's not such a bad idea." Jenna

licked her spoon, "we could do a big community event, get everyone involved. Maybe the mayor would let us use the town hall, free of charge."

"Town hall? How big do you expect this to be?" I gulped, starting to regret my suggestion.

"Like you said, a community event. Something to pull everyone together and celebrate being alive. Not long ago we had the trouble with the rift, then we lost Del and Tiny, then Edith, and of course Roxanne and Carson. That's a lot of death and the whole Carson Singh killing Tiny thing sent shockwaves through the community. It's been a lot to process. A bit of light, laughter, and dancing could go a long way to healing this town."

Jackson reached across the table and entwined his fingers with mine. "She's got a point. I know you have flashbacks to the Christmas Ball in East Dondure, I know why you don't want a party, but how about replacing that bad memory with a good one? Here. With us. With people who love you."

Damn it, he had me. I turned to mush. "Okay, fine." I capitulated as gracefully as I could. "Let's have a big ass event that everyone will talk about for years to come." Staring around the table my heart swelled. Jackson was right. These were my people. I was exactly where I needed to be. Gran and her tenuous career as a teacher of advanced potions at Drixworths Academy for Witches and Wizardry. Jenna and her super reporting skills for the Whitefall Cove Tribune and my best friend since childhood. Monica, my vampire best friend who wasn't with us today because of her severe sun allergy, and Jackson. My love. The man who persuaded my heart that it could love again after the painful beating it took thanks to my ex-fiancée. And of course, Archie, who was currently under my chair, eating the tiny pieces of pie I kept secretly feeding him.

Despite everything that had happened, life at this moment was pretty much perfect. I crossed my fingers under the table and prayed it would stay that way, at least for the weekend!

THE END

If you enjoyed this story, you may enjoy the Gravestone Mysteries. Check out book one,
Fur the Hex of It: www.JaneHinchey.com/Gravestone

Don't want to miss out on new release news? Join my newsletter here: www.JaneHinchey.com/subscribe

Thank you for reading! If you enjoyed this book, I'd greatly appreciate your review.

You can find a complete list of my books, including series and reading order on my website at:

www.JaneHinchey.com

Join my newsletter here:

www.JaneHinchey.com/subscribe

And finally, join my readers group on Facebook here:

www.JaneHinchey.com/LittleDevils

Thank you so much for taking a chance and reading my book . It's readers like you who make this journey worthwhile and fuel my passion for storytelling. Your support means the world to me, and I can't wait to share more exciting stories with you in the future.

xoxo
Jane

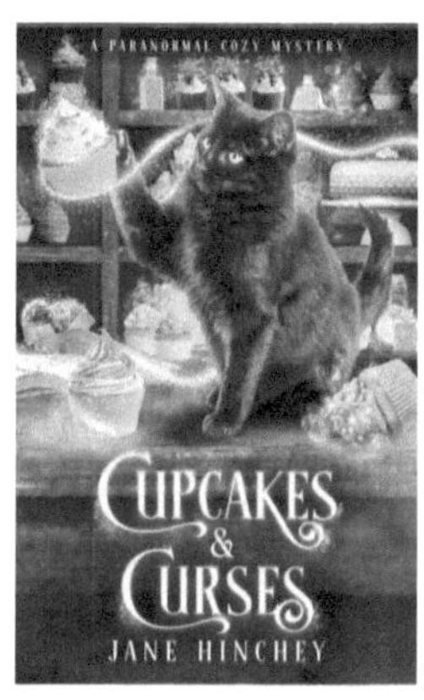

FREE BOOK OFFER

Want to get an email alert when a new book is released?

Sign up for my newsletter today,

https://janehinchey.com/subscribe

and as a bonus, receive a FREE e-book of

Cupcakes & Curses!

READ MORE BY JANE

Find them all at www.JaneHinchey.com/books

<u>The Ghost Detective Mysteries</u>

#1 Ghost Mortem

#2 Give up the Ghost

#3 The Ghost is Clear

#4 A Ghost of a Chance

#5 Here Ghost Nothing

#6 Who Ghost There?

#7 Wild Ghost Chase

#8 Easy Come, Easy Ghost

#9 Life Ghost On

<u>Witch Way Paranormal Cozy Mystery Series</u>

#1 Witch Way to Magic & Mayhem

#2 Witch Way to Romance & Ruin

#3 Witch Way Down Under

#4 Witch Way to Beauty & the Beach

#5 Witch Way to Death & Destruction

#6 Witch Way to Secrets & Sorcery

<u>**The Gravestone Mysteries**</u>

#1 Fur the Hex of it

#2 Battle of the Hexes

#3 What the Hex

<u>**The Midnight Chronicles**</u>

#1 One Minute to Midnight

#2 Two Minutes Past Midnight

#3 Third Strike of Midnight

<u>**Clean Scene Inc.**</u>

#1 All in Vein

PARANORMAL ROMANCE/URBAN FANTASY

The Awakening Trilogy

Hell's Angel Trilogy

The Enforcer Series (4 books)

Standalones

Returned

Secret Fates

Destiny's Touch

Blood Cursed

Heart of Darkness

About Jane

Hi there! I'm Jane, crafting tales of paranormal cozy mysteries sprinkled with urban fantasy romance. Between sips of coffee and dodging my mischievous cats, I immerse myself in stories where magic meets everyday life.

Once known as Zahra Stone in the world of steamy urban fantasy, I've now merged those fiery tales under the Jane Hinchey banner. Off the page you'll find me binging on true crime documentaries or sneaking in a Power Nap. Dive into my stories and join me on an enchanting journey!

Find me here: www.janehinchey.com

facebook.com/janehincheyauthor

instagram.com/janehincheyauthor

amazon.com/Jane-Hinchey/e/B0193449MI

bookbub.com/authors/jane-hinchey

goodreads.com/jane_hinchey